FATHER FINDER

BLOOD OF THE VAMPIRE HUNTER
BOOK FIVE

ID JOHNSON

For my Family

CONTENTS

1

Jo

Voices filtered down the hall as Jo McReynolds stepped out of the shower and began to dry off. After a long day at the training facility, where she not only helped to whip some of the new recruits into shape but also spent several hours working out herself, she'd definitely needed a shower. Not only had she been dripping in sweat when she dragged herself up to the penthouse apartment she'd been sharing with her mother, brother, and sometimes Zane since her mom had returned from the Blood Moon portal about a week ago, but she also just needed some time to herself.

In that week, so much had changed, and yet a lot of things were still the same. Hunters and Guardians had been taking out Vampires by the droves since Holland was no longer around to make the bloodsuckers so fucking strong. The good guys were all training and doing their best to get stronger while rebuilding what had been taken from them during the Revelation. Her brother was still a jealous prick, though recently he'd been paying a lot of attention to that Mallory chick. And the hole in her heart she'd developed when her mother had been taken from her ten years ago was still there. Only now, it was shaped like her dad.

Jo tried not to eavesdrop as she got dressed, but it was hard. Her "funcle" Elliott's voice boomed through the apartment, reaching her ears no matter how hard she tried not to listen. It was clear he was trying to talk her mother, Cadence, into opening the Blue Moon portal to see if her dad, Aaron, might want to come out. From what she could tell, her mother didn't think it was a good idea.

Jo tended to agree. Running a towel through her short, dark hair with blue highlights, she caught a glimpse of herself in the mirror. The comparison to her mother was obvious. They had the same shaped face, same mouth, similar noses. But the blue eyes staring back at her were all her father's.

Biting back a sob, Jo reminded herself that she needed to be tough. She hung her towel on a hook and quietly opened the bathroom door. No matter how hard Elliott tried to convince them to open the portal, it wouldn't matter. In the end, Aaron McReynolds would never come through it. He cared far too much about the fate of humanity to do something so selfish.

"Don't you at least want to say hello?" Elliott was asking her mother as Jo crept her way down the hallway. She didn't intend to eavesdrop, but then, she'd already heard most of the conversation, and she didn't want them to know that either. She was stuck between a rock and… another rock.

"You know I'd love to see him," Cadence said with a sigh. "But it might just make it harder. In the past few days, I've finally started to wrap my mind around the fact that I won't be seeing him again for a while. If I do, it'll make it all that much harder to start over again."

"Bullshit," Elliott proclaimed. "It's going to be hard either way. Ain't it, Jo?"

"Fuck." Cursing under her breath, she stepped around the corner. "I wasn't trying to listen in, but damn, Elliott, your voice is so fucking loud."

He shrugged. It was no secret to him. "I'm not trying to keep my feelings under wrap. I think we need to make sure he's all right, that he got to 'the beyond' in one piece."

Shaking her head, Jo took a seat in an uncomfortable chair near the couch where her mother and her long-time friend were seated. "We know that he did. It's not possible *not* to get there in one piece. Right, Mom?" In the last few days, her mother had been talking a lot about her own experiences in 'the beyond.' She'd told Jo and her twin brother, Cadon, all about how she'd died destroying a powerful Vampire named Daunator, and it had been their father's love, and the memory that she was pregnant with the two of them, that had guided her back to this life. Jo had heard a lot of those stories as a child, but it was a nice reminder. Her mother had seen so many people that had passed away, including Jo's half-sister, the baby her father's first wife had lost before she was born. To think of her father somewhere with his other daughter made her smile–though it also made her a little jealous. He'd never got to hold her in this life.

"I think we should leave him be," she said in solidarity with her mother. "He won't want to come back, not when there's a chance he could bring Holland or someone worse with him."

"What if we can find a way to make sure he doesn't?" Elliott held up a finger, like he'd just had a stroke of genius.

Snorting, Cadence said, "That's not possible."

"It might be. Christian has spent a lot of time in those tunnels. He knows how to get to hell. Maybe he knows of a way we can make sure no one is able to escape when the portal opens."

It was Jo's turn to question his sanity. "You, of all people, are proposing we put our faith in Christian Henry?" Christian had always been some sort of freak show, but it seemed he'd just gotten crazier when Cadence went missing. He'd had feelings for Jo's mother for decades, and the constant years of searching for her in the tunnels of the Blood Moon portal had obviously made him even more insane.

Elliott shrugged one shoulder. "If that's what it takes."

"Why do you want him back so badly?" Jo countered. "I know he was your best friend, but you're an old dude. You have other friends. Didn't you survive for a couple of hundred years without my dad?"

"I'm not that old, thank you very much," Elliott countered. "I'm not even a hundred yet. Your father was more than a friend to me. He was like a brother. And I... I want to tell him that..." Elliott swallowed hard, and Cadence reached over and put her hand on his arm.

"I want to talk to him, too, Elliott. I just think now isn't a good time. It's too soon. I won't be able to rationally speak with him without trying to convince him to come through the portal."

"And if he comes through, we could very well be back to square one," Jo reminded him. "I really don't want to have to fight fucking Holland again so soon."

Elliott's bright green eyes narrowed, but for once, he didn't say anything, only looked away. Jo would've liked to think this might be the end of it, but she knew him better than that. He wasn't being quiet because he'd given up; he was scheming. And that was always dangerous.

Pushing up out of the chair, she stretched her back. "I'm going to go check in with Ashley. She sent me an IAC message a bit ago that we had a lot more new recruits showing up today. Some of them are within range of being changed."

"Let me know if you need anything, honey." Cadence gave her a grateful smile and took a sip of what appeared to be tea. Jo smiled back and headed out the door.

Her mother hadn't wanted to jump right back in as Hunter Leader, and Jo couldn't blame her. She'd lost ten years of her life while she was trapped in the Blood Moon portal, and that place could fuck with a person's mind. So Jo and Cadon were taking care of a lot of the leadership responsibilities, with the help of Ashley Joplin, a Hunter who had stayed behind to get the LIGHTS facilities back up and running while the McReynolds twins were off leading missions. Ashley's husband, Jamie, who was an incredibly strong Healer and also a Guardian, was heading up that side of business at the moment since there was no longer a Guardian Leader.

Jo stepped onto the elevator and let out a deep breath, missing her dad again. That had been Aaron's job for longer than Jo knew, and with him gone, everything could've fallen into chaos.

But it hadn't. He'd trained enough of them to be able to step in and do what needed to be done that they were making it work.

The sound of hammers and the scent of fresh paint hit her lungs as she stepped off the elevator. Not only were they making it work, they were beginning to thrive again. Now that the governments around the world had started to recognize that Vampires were evil and needed to be killed, they were calling on LIGHTS to help. For years, Hunters and Guardians had been hunted down and killed or imprisoned. Now, finally, they were able to do their job again.

Jo made her way over to the wall next to the door where a man she knew well was directing a few others in hanging up a new sign. In large white letters, it read "LIGHTS: Lincoln International Guardian and Hunter Training Station." A smile slipped into place just seeing it there in the apartment complex where most of the staff lived.

"What do you think, Miss Jo?" Juan Diego asked, gesturing at his crew's work. "It looks good, no?"

"It looks amazing, my friend." She wrapped an arm around him and gave him a squeeze. "You always do good work."

"Well, now that you have made me in charge of all of the facilities, I can make sure everything looks the best." He grinned at her, and she patted him on the back again. Juan had come to work for them before she was even born, and he always did a great job, no matter what he was asked to do. She was glad he'd survived the Revelation and was back. "You should check out the big sign out front."

"I will do that," she promised him, continuing toward the door.

"Tomorrow, I will work on the fountain."

Jo stopped in her tracks and took a deep breath. Sometimes, she had difficulty understanding Juan Diego because of his heavy accent, but she was pretty sure she heard that correctly. Slowly, she turned to face him. "The little girl with the watering can?"

"That's the one." He nodded.

Forcing a smile to her face, she managed, "That's great. Thank you. I know it would mean a lot to my father."

"He was a good man." A tear formed quickly in the corner of Juan

Diego's eye. Jo understood just how fast that could happen when one thought of the deceased Guardian Leader. "The best."

"Yes, he was." She pivoted and headed out the door before she was able to form another tear. A strong wind was blowing, which helped relieve her of that overwhelming sensation that she needed to cry, but as she made her way to the facility where Ashley and Jamie were meeting and assessing the new recruits, her mind lingered on the fountain she'd been able to see from her bedroom window since she was a little girl.

"Who is that girl, Daddy?"

"That is your sister. Her name is Aarolyn,"

"But I can't have a rock sister."

"No, she's not a rock. She's in heaven with her mother, a nice woman named Aislyn. They died a long time ago, and then I met your mother, and now I have another little girl."

Her father had kissed her on the top of the head and changed the subject, and that was that.

After all these years, Aaron was in heaven with Aislyn and Aarolyn, and Jo selfishly wished that when she pushed through that door to greet the Guardian Leader it would be him instead of Jamie.

Maybe she was more human than she liked to admit.

2

Cadon

"Push up on your tiptoes and then jump." Cadon demonstrated for Mallory, not for the first time, the best way for her to grab the bar dangling six feet above her head. Most of the time, Hunters wouldn't have any problem at all leaping six feet into the air, but Mallory was new to this.

And if Cadon was being honest with himself, Mallory wasn't just new—she wasn't very good.

A lot of reasons for this sprang to his head. After all, she'd been imprisoned in Alcatraz for almost half of her life. It wasn't like the Vampires gave their captives a lot of opportunity to get the exercise they required on a daily basis. In fact, Mallory had mentioned a couple of days ago that she'd only been outside a couple of times since she was imprisoned, and that was when the vampires were changing her to another cell block.

He couldn't imagine not being able to see the sky for years at a time.

"I'm trying," Mallory told him with a grunt of frustration, "but I just can't reach it." She jumped up again, and her fingers nearly swiped the bar before she landed back on the gym floor with a huff.

Cadon took a deep breath and reassessed the situation. She'd been working out for almost two hours now. Maybe she was tired. He pushed the memory of the fact that she hadn't been able to reach it earlier that day out of his mind. "Why don't we call it a day and try again tomorrow?"

Her violet eyes met his gaze, and her bottom lip began to quiver as she managed to say, "Okay."

Seeing that she was distraught, Cadon put a hand on her shoulder. "Hey, you're doing great, Mal. Don't be upset."

"I'm not doing great," she countered. "I suck at this."

"No, you don't. You're good at… running."

"I'm unbelievably slow and almost flew off the treadmill twice."

"But you didn't." He gave her a crooked grin. "And you ran just as long as I did."

"True."

He didn't mention that he'd already ran thirty miles before she showed up for her training session. "Listen, Mal, no one ever said this was going to be easy. It's not. But you'll be just fine. We'll get you trained up, and you'll be ready to defend yourself if there's ever an attack here at headquarters where you'll be working." Mallory had already made it clear to him that she did not want to be out in the field. She'd said that she'd already encountered enough Vampires to last the rest of her life, and since that was likely to be close to another 200 years, she was done.

Cadon and Jo agreed there were plenty of work opportunities for Mallory in an office setting where she wouldn't have to go out and fight Vampires, but she did need basic training.

And eventually, she was going to need an IAC, but since that could be painful, he hadn't pressed the issue.

"I'll see you tomorrow," Cadon assured her. "Same bat time, same bat place?"

Mallory's forehead scrunched up. "What?"

Feeling his face flush, Cadon admitted, "I honestly have no idea what that means. It's just something I heard my dad and Elliott say sometimes."

"Oh. We should search it up. Yeah, same time–and place." Mallory left out the "bat" business.

Giving her another smile, Cadon dropped his hand and let her go. Watching her walk away felt a little bit like checking out her ass for a few minutes, so he turned his attention to a basketball game that was going on at the other end of the court.

"Wanna play?" Scott Joplin, his best friend since he was a kid, shouted to him.

"No, thanks."

Taking advantage of his distracted state, Amanda Sanderson, Elliott's daughter, stole the ball from Scott and drove down the court slamming it into the hoop. The other players on her team cheered while Scott's side chastised him for being distracted.

With a chuckle, Cadon turned and headed to the men's locker room to take a shower. His sister had sent him an IAC message earlier that she was going to check in with Ashley and Jamie, and he figured it wouldn't hurt for him to do the same. They'd gotten so many new recruits in the last few days that they were beginning to run out of rooms in the apartment complex used for newbies. They needed to figure out what to do about it.

When he walked into the locker room, the scent of old gym socks hit him first, followed by a puff of steam, and the sound of someone humming "Drunken Sailor." Swearing under his breath, Cadon decided to make this as quick as possible. He knew who the hummer was, and he'd just as soon avoid him at all costs.

He'd just taken off his shirt when the shower turned off and Christian Henry walked out, buck naked and dripping. Averting his eyes, Cadon said, "Do you need a towel?"

"I prefer to air dry," the old Guardian replied. He hadn't shaved in a while, and he was beginning to look like a pirate himself. "What are you up to, McReynolds?"

Not daring to lower his eyes, Cadon said, "Just getting cleaned up to go meet with Jamie."

"Oh. That sounds… boring." Christian began grabbing his clothes out of his locker, still refusing to dry off with a towel.

Seeing no point in agreeing or disagreeing, Cadon headed to the shower and turned it on before stepping out of his pants away from Christian. He'd never been comfortable around that dude, but ever since his final trip out of the Blood Moon portal, he'd seemed even weirder somehow.

Cadon had just gotten a good lather under the rainfall shower head when he heard another familiar voice. Dax Forrest greeted Christian in a much friendlier tone than Cadon would've ever used, so he had to imagine the Guardian was wearing pants now. They chatted for a bit, and the conversation turned to recent rescues. "We just need to find out what happened to Hannah," Dax lamented.

A chuckle reverberated around the locker room before Christian said, "Don't hold your breath."

Alarmed, Caden tuned into the conversation even more closely.

"What do you mean?" Dax asked, also clearly thinking that was an odd response.

"I mean… I think she's dead," Christian replied. "No activity on her IAC. I can't force it on. She's either dead or buried somewhere."

"Buried somewhere?" Dax questioned. "You mean like how Daunator buried you? Is that still a thing?"

"Don't know. Don't care." Christian started to hum again, and it sounded to Cadon like he was leaving.

Dax didn't let him. "I thought you and Hannah were friends."

Cadon had thought the same thing. While it was hard for him to believe anyone could like Christian, he wasn't aware of any bad blood between the two of them.

Christian laughed again. "Forrest, you should know by now I don't have any fucking friends. And that's fine by me." The humming picked up and then faded behind the closing of the door.

"You're a real asshole, Christian Henry," Dax mumbled.

Cadon wanted to agree, but he didn't want Dax to know he'd been eavesdropping. He finished his shower about the time Dax started his, grabbed a towel, and headed over to get dressed.

There'd been a lot going on since Holland died, but Dax wasn't wrong. They needed to make finding out what had happened to Hannah Roberts a priority. She'd been second in command to his father, and it wasn't right to leave her hanging. If she was dead, they needed to know that, too.

Deciding he needed to bring it up with his sister, who was still in charge, and Jamie, he slipped on his shoes, shoved his gym pants in his bag along with the rest of his smelly clothes and stepped out the door—running right into Mallory.

The collision sent her careening. Cadon reached out and steadied her. She looked up at him with narrowed violet eyes. "Maybe you watch where you're going?" It was clear she was irritated, but she didn't have a mean bone in her body.

"So sorry." It had been an accident, one neither of them could've avoided without X-ray vision, a trick Cadon's father had been good at, but it wasn't hereditary.

She relaxed a little. "It's okay." Mallory glanced over at where his hand still rested on her arm. "You can let go."

"Right." He hadn't wanted to. She smelled like jasmine and honeysuckle. Even when she was sweaty from working out, she looked great, but now that she'd had a shower, letting go was the last thing he wanted to do.

Clearing his throat, he ran his hand through his hair and scratched the back of his neck. Mallory's eyes widened as she seemed to try to figure out what the hell was the matter with him. Since Cadon wasn't about to admit he'd been thinking about her as more than just his newest trainee, he took a step backward.

"See you tomorrow." Mallory smiled at him, and then headed back toward the exit, where she'd obviously been heading before he nearly knocked her over.

She was almost all the way through the door when he managed to mutter, "See you tomorrow."

Laughter erupted from the entryway to the gym. "You love her," Amanda said in a sing-song voice.

"I do not." Cadon glared at her, wishing he was the one holding the basketball instead of his uncle's sister so he could throw it at her. He wasn't exactly sure what their relationship was since she was his aunt's husband's sister, but sometimes she felt like a pesky sibling.

Scott came up behind Amanda wearing the same teasing grin, and Cadon gave up. Mumbling a curse word at them, he headed for the door.

Outside, he took a deep breath and tried to clear his head. He could see Mallory walking toward the apartment building in the distance and had the overwhelming urge to stand there and watch her walk away, but that seemed a little creepy once he thought it through. Instead, he headed toward the office building where Jamie and Ashley were greeting the new recruits, knowing his sister was probably still there as well, even though it had been a while since she'd messaged him.

He walked in to find several strangers sitting in chairs in a makeshift lobby that was really just a hallway. He nodded hello to them, trying not to be impolite, and then looked through the glass in Jamie's office door. Ashley, Jo, and another girl were all inside with the Healer. The stranger was sitting on a table while Jamie shined a light in her eyes.

His sister saw him standing there and motioned for him to come in. "I don't want to interrupt," Cadon said quietly as he walked inside.

"It's fine," Jamie assured him over his shoulder. "Just making sure Jingsha here is healthy enough for her Transformation serum." The girl on the table, who looked to be in her late teens, smiled uncomfortably.

Cadon lifted a hand in her direction and then walked over to Ashley and Jo. "Should we be in here?"

"He's not getting a break anytime soon," Ashley explained. "I called Cale on the IAC and asked him if he could come down and take over. That was a while ago, and he's not here yet."

"Is something going on with him?" Cadon asked. They were all speaking in hushed tones so they didn't disturb Jamie with his patient. "He seemed grouchy on our mission."

"He's always grouchy," Jo noted. "Not that I'm one to talk."

"I'm not sure," Ashley admitted. "I would think he'd be happy since your mom is back."

"Everyone should be," Cadon replied. "But the way you said that…. Is there a reason why he would be happier than, say, Dax or Aurora?"

Ashley made a face and opened her mouth to speak when the office door opened, and Dr. Cale Ryan walked in, a scowl on his face. He wore a lab coat and had a stethoscope wrapped around his neck. "Well, here I am. Back for another shift, even though I just left here a few hours ago."

"Thank goodness we don't sleep much." Jamie turned to give him a smile, but also a bit of a cutting look, as if to tell him to knock it off. "Jingsha is ready for her shot. There are about six other people waiting in the hallway."

"For now. There'll be another seventy after that. What are we going to do when the apartments are full? We can't take everyone." Cale didn't seem to care that one of the problem patients was sitting right there.

"That is exactly what the four of us need to meet to speak about," Jamie replied, motioning to where Cadon and the others stood. "So thank you so much for coming down."

Shaking his head, Cale grumbled again and stepped over to where the now frightened Jingsha awaited him.

Letting out a sigh, Jamie said, "Why don't we meet in Christian's office if he's not there? And if he is, we'll go to what used to be the conference room, even though it's still a bit of a mess."

They all agreed and headed out the hall. When Cadon heard the first refrain of "Drunken Sailor," he said, "Conference room?" and they all shifted direction. One thing none of them needed to deal with at the moment was the crazy Guardian who thought he was a pirate.

3

Jo

"WE DON'T HAVE enough manpower or resources right now to build another building, but we could potentially take the complex where we used to house Vampires and turn that into a facility for new recruits," Ashley was saying, pointing at the building in question on a map she'd gone back to grab out of Jamie's office after they'd made it into the conference room. "There's plenty of room there, though it's in about as good a shape as this room."

Jo looked around. It was hard to believe this was where her parents used to hold their briefings. They'd managed to find a table and a few chairs that were in good enough shape to use for their purposes, but the rest of the room was a wreck with overturned tables, holes in the walls, and wires hanging where their projector used to fit in the ceiling.

"That might work," Jamie said, scratching his chin. "But a lot of those rooms were more like cells. They might not be the most comfortable."

"A lot of these people won't be here long-term," Ashley pointed out. "Some of them have already Transformed naturally and just want training while others need the shot and then training, but ultimately, we'll need to assign them to teams and send them back out into the rest of the world. There are still a lot of pockets of Vampires out there, and since most of them don't have trackers anymore, like we were used to back in the day, it's going to take more of us to find them."

Jo remembered the days of Vampires being fitted with trackers so her father and the other Guardians knew where they were at all times. During the Revelation, it became illegal to track Vampires. Now, of course, with President Crimson in hiding and the American federal government trying to reorganize without Vampires, laws would be changed back to the way they used to be before humans knew Vampires existed.

So long as another powerful Vampire didn't come along and shift the situation back to their favor.

"Jo?" Jamie said her name like it wasn't the first time. "Do you think that will work?"

"The Vampire holding facility?" she asked. He nodded. At least she hadn't been completely tuned out. "Yeah, I think so. If it's not all that comfy, then those people will work harder to get the hell out of here."

"At least there's not still blood all over the walls," Ashley muttered.

Cadon and Jo exchanged glances. "What?" her brother asked.

"Surely you guys have heard about Bonnie?" Jamie asked. "The little girl Vampire who wreaked havoc over there when your mom first took over as Hunter Leader?"

"Bonnie? That happened in that building?" Jo's eyes widened. She'd heard a bit about the sweet looking little girl that had killed a number of Hunters and did an unbelievable amount of damage to her father before they'd managed to find and kill her, but she didn't remember all the details. Her parents' Vampire hunting stories had often been white noise to her when she was growing up. She'd always figured she'd hear them again someday. Then, her mother was gone, and now her father was dead, and she wished she would've listened better.

"Yeah. That's one Vampire I hope stays dead," Ashley said, shaking her head. "All right. I think that will work. I'll get with Juan Diego and see how long it will take to modify that building. We need to talk about Grand Central Station."

Jo nodded. "I'm planning to call a meeting with the experienced LIGHTS members tomorrow to organize a New York trip for next week. I'm thinking I'll ask Elliott to lead it."

"Next week?" Jamie echoed. "You're not going to get Elliott to leave your mom's side next week."

Pursing her lips, Jo contemplated what he was saying. "I was actually thinking it might be best if Elliott wasn't with Mom during the blue moon. Less chances of persuading her to do something she doesn't want to do."

Ashley and Jamie exchanged a glance that made Jo think they might be using the IAC. Or they might just know what the other is thinking because they'd been married for so long. Jamie spoke again. "Are you sure that your mom doesn't want to do it?"

Remembering what she'd heard that morning when she was unintentionally eavesdropping, Jo shrugged. "I know that my dad doesn't want to come back, and–"

"*Our* dad," Cadon inserted, looking slightly annoyed.

Jo glared at him. "*Our* dad. And Mom–*our* mom–doesn't want to put him in a position where he feels like he has to choose." Once again, she thought of his family on the other side. A sting of jealousy pulsed through her chest, but she had to let it go. Her baby sister never even knew her father. Now, she'd finally get to be with him. It seemed selfish for her to want to talk him into coming back to this life when everything was perfect there.

How perfect can it be for him without Mom?

But then, he wouldn't remember their mother. He wouldn't remember any of them.

"Don't you think he'd want to know that you found her?" Ashley asked.

Shaking her head, Jo said, "Mom told us that she didn't remember anything while she was there. Elliott said the same. I have no idea what Christian remembered, and I'm not going to ask, but there's no point in reminding him of her if he doesn't have to think about her right now."

Once again, Jamie and Ashley exchanged a look she couldn't read. Jamie turned back to Jo. "Have you ever tried to get Elliott to do something he doesn't want to do?"

Jo's eyebrows shot up as she considered the question. "I once made him give me a Cheeto he didn't want to part with."

Snickering, the healer shook his head. "While it's always hard to get Elliott to part with his food, that's not what I mean. Getting him to go on a mission he doesn't want to go on is going to be nearly impossible. If you push it, you're going to have to fight him on it."

"Literally fight him?" Cadon laughed. "Now, that's something I'd like to see."

"I can take him," Jo said calmly, imagining herself in a wrestling ring with the burly Guardian. "He's bigger than me, but I'm faster."

"He won't fight you," Jamie assured her. "But he will be the biggest pain in the ass you could ever imagine. I don't think it's a good idea to push for that. I'd wait. You're going to want to keep an eye on him during the blue moon."

"It's fine. I'll just hide Dad," Jo said with another rock of her shoulders.

That sent Ashley and Jamie into a fit of laughter she didn't understand. "Do you really think that Elliott hasn't already hidden him?" Jamie finally managed to get out.

With her eyebrows practically touching, Jo turned to her brother. He looked just as confused. "What?" he asked.

"When Elliott was in 'the beyond,'" Jamie began, through his laughter, "your parents fought over whether or not to get him back. Your mother hid Elliott from your dad and replaced him with ashes from the fireplace. He had no idea. I've never seen anyone pull one over on your dad before."

Her mouth dropped open. "I had no idea," Jo muttered.

"Yeah, so I seriously doubt that's even your dad in that urn for now. Elliott probably has him in his underwear drawer or something, just in case someone tries to pull the old switcheroo on him," Jamie continued.

"How did Mom pull that off?" Cadon asked.

Jo mumbled, "*Our* mom," and glared at him.

"Oh, knock it off." Cadon batted at her, but Jo grabbed his arm and twisted.

"All right. Knock it off." Ashley used her mom voice, and they both stopped. "It's like you're twelve again."

"He's always been twelve." Jo stuck her tongue out at her brother, but he just shook his head.

"She pulled it off with Christian's help," Jamie said loudly enough to be heard over all the racket. "No one thought she'd get him to help her, so it was the perfect plan."

Somewhere in the back of her mind, an idea sparked, one Jo couldn't quite get a grasp on. "Christian?" she repeated. A shiver threatened to come up her spine, but she stopped it.

"That's right," Jamie said with a sharp nod. "The one and only Major Henry."

"He's such an ass." Cadon shook his head and folded his arms. "In the shower earlier today, Dax was asking him if he had any idea where Hannah might be, and he didn't even care."

"Why were you taking a shower with Dax and Christian?" Jo blurted. "Gross."

Again, Cadon swung at her. "The showers. In the locker room. You're disgusting."

"You said it."

"I honestly like to hear you guys arguing again," Jamie chimed in. "At least you're talking."

Jo turned and glared at her brother. The Healer had a point. For years, they hadn't spoken to one another at all. Now, she could tease her brother about having a three-way with a lanky old man and a crazy Guardian everyone hated.

"We do need to find Hannah," Ashley agreed. "But first, we need to figure out what to do about the blue moon. Whatever your mom wants, we'll support her." She reached over and took Jamie's hand, and he nodded.

Jo knew she'd have to get a real answer from her mother, and soon, before the blue moon rose over the horizon, and they were out of time.

The door opened, and Aunt Cassidy walked in. "Hey, sorry to interrupt, but we have a problem."

"Just one?" Jamie teased.

Cassidy gave him a sarcastic grin and turned to Jo. "We've got about three hundred Vampires messaging me from the surrounding area asking for asylum. They all say they never chose this life and don't want to be turned. Can we put them in the old facility where we used to house Vampires?"

"The one we just decided to use for Guardians and Hunters?" Jo asked, looking at Ashley, who nodded.

"Fuck," Cassidy mumbled. "Isn't there anywhere else we can put them?"

Jo realized every eye in the room was on her. Maybe she should try to talk her dad into coming back. He would've already had this handled—and she had absolutely no fucking idea what to do.

4

Cadon

Back in the penthouse, Cadon enjoyed the silence for a few moments. His sister had called for his mother to go help Cass figure out where to house the newly arriving Vampires, so he had a few moments without anyone else around to disturb his thoughts.

Cracking open a beer, he stared into the refrigerator for a while. Ashley had done a great job of making sure the grocery store downstairs was restocked, but with Elliott spending so much time at their place, it seemed like they were out of food all the time. He grabbed the necessary items to make himself a turkey and cheese sandwich and set them on the counter.

As he made his sandwich, his mind went back over everything Jamie and Ashley had said. The new recruits were a good thing–the Hunters and Guardians, not the Vampires. He could do without those. Back in the day, his parents had decided all Vampires needed to die, and he wished they could go back to that philosophy now, but it seemed like Aunt Cass, who was half-Vampire, was advocating to take these "innocent" bloodsuckers in. He wasn't willing to die on that sword at the moment. But having new recruits to train and get ready for the field should be helpful when they finally went to Vampire strongholds like New York.

It irritated the hell out of him that Margie Joplin, Jamie's sister, hadn't taken out Grand Central station the way she promised she would when Cadon was leading the rescue mission to Alcatraz. Why Margie hadn't done her job, he still didn't know. She was so important to the Australian Army that he hadn't dared to ask. If Jamie knew, he didn't say, but then the siblings had never gotten along.

Cadon put the sandwich fixings away and headed to the living room with his snack and his beer. He liked the taste of this particular brand of alcohol, though it did nothing for him or most Hunters and Guardians. It was just something people his age did—relax with a beer.

He sat in the uncomfortable chair by the sofa and only tolerated it for a second before he got up and moved to the couch. That chair had to go. He didn't know anyone who liked it.

His thoughts returned to Mallory. If the other recruits ended up being as hopeless as she was, they were all in trouble. But he didn't think they would be. She was just so sweet and innocent, it was difficult for her to learn the tactics necessary to defend herself and potentially kill off the Vampires that threatened to kill her should she ever find herself in a battle.

He hoped that never happened. She'd been terrified during the escape from Alcatraz, as she should've been considering she was the only human involved, save the boat captain who didn't step foot on land. He probably would've been scared, too.

But now, she'd transformed and was a Hunter, like him. She should've been strong, fast, and confident. Yet, her timidity continued to make her more vulnerable than she should be, and he couldn't imagine her ever going out in the field. They could find a job for her back at headquarters, but if he couldn't find a way to help her to learn to keep herself safe, and something happened to her, he'd never forgive himself.

His eye caught the urn on top of the fireplace mantel, and immediately, the image of his father filled his mind's eye. A smile on his face, Aaron McReynolds always looked calm, confident, and collected, so that's how his son pictured him now. When everyone else was losing their shit, his dad always knew exactly what to do.

Finishing his beer, Cadon set his can down and dragged himself up off the couch, stepping over to the urn Elliott had placed there not long after his family had moved back into the penthouse where he grew up. It was hard to believe his father was inside that tiny container. He knew the important part–his dad's soul–couldn't be encapsulated in any sort of container, but it was hard to imagine someday having his own body burned down to small enough contents to fit inside something of that nature.

He remembered what Jamie had said about Elliott potentially fucking around with his dad's ashes so he wasn't actually in the urn at all. Surely, that was just a joke on Jamie's part, and no one would do such a thing. Yet, he had the feeling the story about his mom tricking his dad wasn't a joke.

Glancing over his shoulder, Cadon took a look around the living room. No one else was in the apartment. He was sure of that. His sister and mom were gone, so it was just him. Carefully, he picked up the urn and took the lid off, staring inside. It looked like ashes to him. Whether it was his father or the remnants of a barbecue, he couldn't say. Leaning even closer, he took a whiff. Did he smell... hotdogs?

"You okay there, kid?"

The sound of Elliott's deep voice behind him caught Cadon off guard. He fumbled the urn and the lid, almost dropping both of them before managing to get a grip on both. Quickly, he set the urn back on the mantel and put the lid on it before turning around, his heart beating out of his chest.

"What the fuck, Elliott?" Cadon dragged his hands down his jeans, his palms suddenly feeling sweaty. "You scared the shit out of me."

"Sorry. Didn't mean to." The burly Guardian crossed his arms across his barrel chest. "What were you doing there?"

"Nothing."

Elliott raised one eyebrow.

"Shit, why the fuck do I think I have to answer to you? I'm twenty-five years old, and you're not my dad." He looked at the urn. He wasn't completely convinced the ashes in that jar were either.

"You seem a little defensive." Elliott relaxed a little bit. "Everything okay?"

"I'm fine." Dragging a hand through his hair, he returned to the couch and picked up his empty beer can, taking it into the kitchen to throw it away before grabbing another one. He didn't bother to offer Elliott one, knowing he'd take whatever he wanted to.

Cadon opened the beer and took a long draw before turning to see Elliott standing in the doorway to the kitchen. "Did you mess with Dad's ashes?"

"Who you been talking to?" Elliott barked. "Christian? Jamie? Your mom?"

"No one," Cadon lied, pushing past him to get back into the living room. "Dad's ashes smell like hotdogs."

"The man always did love a Ballpark frank. You wouldn't think it by looking at him, but it's true."

Cadon turned and rolled his eyes, knowing that wasn't the case. His dad ate less than a thirteen-year-old girl. He didn't have to eat for some reason. It might've had to do with that weird shot he gave himself that almost killed him, or maybe he was just different than everyone else.

He sank down into the uncomfortable chair by accident before swearing under his breath. Unwilling to admit how much he hated it, he stared at Elliott. "I know Dad didn't like hotdogs."

"Maybe you're smelling me. I ate so much for lunch, I don't remember if I had a frankfurter or ten or not."

"No," Cadon argued. "I think you're hiding something."

"I would never." Elliott sank down onto the couch. "Man, this sofa is comfortable." He stretched his back. "Like sitting on a pillow."

Cadon wanted to tell him to fuck off, but he didn't. Instead, he continued to stare at him for a moment before saying, "I'm pretty sure Jo is sending you to New York. Next week."

Elliott stared back before that deep rumble emanated from his throat again. "The hell she is."

"She's the Hunter Leader right now. If she says you have to go, you have to go."

"I'm a Guardian," Elliott reminded him. "I don't have to do jack shit."

"Jamie will support whatever she says." Cadon wasn't actually sure that was true since Jamie had seemed to think Elliott wouldn't go on the mission if it was during the blue moon, but he didn't mind attempting a bluff.

"Well, if that's the case, I'll quit. I'm not leaving your mom during the blue moon, and she's not ready to go out into the field."

Frustrated, Cadon leaned forward, interlacing his fingers. "He doesn't want to come back. We all know that. Why don't you just let him rest in peace?"

"You don't know him like I do," Elliott countered. "I know he won't want to let anything dangerous back into the world, but he'll want to see your mom. If he decides to come back, so be it."

"But what if Holland comes back?" Cadon felt exasperated. "Or Dracula? Or Daunator?"

Elliott's mouth was already open to argue before Cadon spat out the last name, and he started to laugh. "Daunator? That sounds like a robot potato. It's Daunator, dumbass."

"Excuse me for not being as old as you," Cadon replied with a snarl.

"You don't have to be old to know the history. You and your sister never paid any attention to our stories, and now it's gonna come back to bite you in the ass. All of those creeps already came through the Blue Moon Portal. They're not coming through again."

"You don't know that."

"What are the chances?"

"Too great for Dad to fuck around with!" Cadon ran a hand through his hair, wishing he could just get it into his uncle's skull that his plan was a bad one. "Just leave it be, man."

"Your mom," Elliott said quietly.

"What about her?"

"No, your mom." Elliott nodded to the door a split second before it opened and Cadence came in, followed by Jo and Zane.

How their generation always seemed to know when someone was around, Cadon would never understand. He still had no idea how Elliott had managed to sneak up on him.

"What's going on?" Cadence stood in the middle of the room, looking back and forth between Elliott and Cadon, a smile on her face, but the confusion evident in the way she held her eyebrows.

"We need to settle this blue moon thing once and for all," Cadon blurted, finishing off his second beer. "We have work to do, and if you know for sure you don't want to see Dad, Elliott needs to get his ass to New York with Jo and everyone else who's going, and if you do want to see Dad, we need to make sure we don't let anything through."

"There's no way to prevent something coming through if your father decides to come through the Blue Moon Portal." Cadence crossed the room and sank down on the arm of the couch. "If he doesn't cross, nothing else will."

"You're sure about that?" Cadon questioned. "Nothing can sneak through?"

Cadence shook her head. "No. It's not possible." She looked at Elliott who nodded in agreement. "But if he does come through, we can't keep the Vampires out. One of them will also come, and it has always been a huge problem before. We won't be able to stop it."

"Actually, about that...." Jo was still standing next to her boyfriend by the door. She stared at her mother for a second before glancing at Elliott, Cadon, and Zane before returning her gaze to her mom's eyes. "I have an idea."

Cadon swallowed hard. What the hell had Jo come up with now?

He probably didn't want to know.

5

Jo

EVERY EYE in the room seemed to bore through her face as Jo pondered how to explain the hair-brained idea she'd come up with when she was helping Cass and her mom figure out what to do with the Vampires seeking asylum. Ultimately, they'd decided they didn't have the capacity for that at the moment, and even though Cassidy had been pissed about it, she'd told the bloodsuckers to check back in a few months–if they were still around.

"What's your idea?" Her mother's smile was more comforting than the wide-eyed stare she was getting from her brother. Elliott just had that skeptical, snide expression on his face, and she hadn't dared to turn her head to look at Zane because she didn't need to know if he disapproved of her speaking up. They still hadn't quite sorted everything out since their journey through the portal together. He was her boyfriend–sort of–and that was good enough for now. Why monkey with that?

"Well, since the last time the Blue Moon Portal opened, Christian has figured out a lot about the Blood Moon Portal and how the

27

gateway to hell and all of that is connected, right?" She wandered over to the smaller of the two couches and sat down across from her mother and Elliott. Zane followed and squeezed in next to her. Cadon looked extremely uncomfortable in that fucking chair that needed to be taken out back, doused with gasoline, and used as an example of what happened to Vampires who didn't play by the rules. They, too, could become flaming torches of indignation.

"Yes, that's true," Elliott said, looking at Cadence who shrugged. "We know a lot more about the tunnels now." He narrowed one eye, giving her a questioning look. "What you gettin' at Jo-Jo?"

She stifled a groan, not wanting to egg him on by reminding him of how much she hated it when he called her that. "Well, what if we sent Christian into hell to make sure nothing comes out when Dad comes through?" There. She'd said it.

The room was completely silent for several seconds as her family members, actual and extended, took into consideration her suggestion. Then, that quiet was shattered by Elliott's deep, boisterous laugh. "Are you shitting me?" he asked. "No fucking way!"

Jo's eyes widened in horror and embarrassment. While she had been expecting a bit of pushback, she didn't think the idea was all that ridiculous. Elliott made it sound like she'd suggested they send a two-year-old in a Hunter Halloween costume to guard the portal.

"Elliott," Cadence scolded, hitting him in the arm hard enough to jar him slightly but not to hurt him. "Don't be a jackass."

"Well, I'm sorry, but she can't be serious. There's no way in fucking hell–pun intended–your father would come through the portal knowing that the one person who hates him more than anyone else in the world was charged with the task of keeping Vampires from entering the earthly plane. I'm sorry. The entire idea is ridiculous." He straightened up slightly, cleared his throat, and said, "Although, I do respect you, Jo. As a person. And a leader." And then he started laughing again.

"Elliott, you're being an ass," Zane said in her defense. "The idea might need some tweaking. Maybe it's not Christian. Maybe it's somebody else."

"Maybe there's no way it will work no matter who we put in there," Cadon chimed in. "I know you guys were just in there, and maybe you think you have an idea of how this all works, but do you really? For all we know, it's some other portal that opens when the Blue Moon Portal opens that just sucks a Vampire right out of hell. We have no idea how it works."

"But we know how to get to hell," Jo reminded her brother with a narrowed gaze. "So it would be possible to keep a better eye on the situation."

"A better eye, of course," Cadence said, the voice of reason. "But, honey, your brother is right. We just don't know enough about how it works to try that. For all we know, Christian could end up trapped in hell forever."

"Suddenly, I am all for this plan." Elliott's demeanor changed entirely. "I say we go for it. Send Christian to hell. Hopefully, he'll get out okay." He sighed. "But one just can never tell what might happen in these types of situations."

Cadence punched him again. "Stop it. Christian spent years in those tunnels looking for me. I'm not going to put him in a situation where he might end up trapped in hell. Even though Aaron and Christian never got along, Aaron wouldn't want that either. They had to have grown closer during their time working together to find me, right?"

"No," Elliott said quickly. "Christian still hates Aaron with every fiber of his being."

"We could at least talk to him and see if he has any ideas." Jo hated to think that her idea was completely useless. "Maybe there's even a back way out of there that Dad could use."

"From 'the beyond'? Honey, I don't think so." Cadence gave her daughter a sympathetic look, and Jo fought the tears that threatened to remind her that she had no fucking idea what she was doing. She just wanted her parents to be together again. To be happy. Like they were before her mom was kidnapped.

"What if it was someone else?" Jo asked. "What if we sent a bunch of people into the tunnels to make sure nothing goes through?"

Cadence shook her head. "That won't work either. Baby, we're just going to have to accept the fact that it'll be up to your dad. If he wants to come back, we'll fight whatever else comes through with him."

Elliott gasped and turned to look at Cadence. "Does that mean… you're going to open the portal?"

Cadence's mouth twitched a few times. Her eyes shifted to the urn sitting on the fireplace mantel. "I think I might," she said. "I just want to tell him I'm okay. Tell him I love him." Turning back to face Elliott, she added, "Of course, that means you're going to have to give me my husband back and take those ashes from your last cookout and dispose of them properly."

"I knew it!" Cadon exclaimed, pointing a finger at Elliott. "I knew Dad smelled like hotdogs!"

Confused, Jo let whatever was happening between them go and turned her attention to the bigger question. "Mom, are you sure? You really want to do that?"

Cadence turned and looked at her before nodding. "I do. But you guys will be there with me, right?" She looked at each of them and waited for a nod, including Zane, who agreed he'd be there with her. "Okay. Then, yes. I want to do it."

Elliott's silent fist pump was enough to let everyone know he felt as if he'd scored a victory.

Jo wasn't so sure. If Elliott was there when that portal opened, he was going to do his damnedest to try to convince her father to come back through, which meant she might need back up anyway. Maybe she needed to talk to Christian after all.

"What's for dinner?" Elliott hopped up, clapping his hands together and rubbing his palms. "Steak? Hamburgers?"

"You need more ashes?" Cadon mumbled, pulling himself up out of the chair. It was clear he was also apprehensive about all of this. "I'm going to meet Scott, Amanda, and some of the other guys at the pizza parlor."

"Have fun, honey." Cadence stood and hugged her son. "It's so nice they got that place open again."

Cadon hugged her back and disappeared. A tinge of jealousy that her brother was still friends with the people they'd grown up with panged in her chest, but she let it go. At least she had Zane.

"I'll eat anything," she said, unwedging herself from the loveseat. "I'm going to go for a walk."

"Be careful." Cadence's words were more out of habit than an actual warning. She smiled at her mom and headed to the door.

In her head, Zane asked through the IAC, *"Do you want company?"*

"I just need to clear my head." She turned to smile at him, and he nodded, but she could see concern behind his eyes.

Maybe he was right to be concerned. Technically, she was the Hunter Leader, so she could do whatever she wanted to, but she'd just had two highly experienced team members tell her that what she was considering doing was a bad idea, and yet, she was still mulling it over.

Jo made it out of the apartment building and was on her way to the offices, not sure if she'd actually go look for Christian or just check in with Jamie when she saw Ryker coming her way. Part of her wanted to turn a corner really quickly to avoid him. The other wanted to stop and shoot the shit. He was different now that he was a Guardian. He was still a dick, but he seemed to have a purpose in life now. He tipped his head at her, and she decided to keep walking in his direction since it was where she'd been going anyway.

"What's up, McReynolds? Any jobs coming our way?" Ryker asked, stopping in front of her.

"We're still working on scheduling New York, but it'll be after the Blue Moon."

He growled. "Is your mom going to open that fucking portal?" It was clear by his tone he'd had enough of portals for a while. Who could blame him?

"I don't think my dad will come through," she assured him.

"I hope not. I want to kill Vampires as badly as the rest of the team, but I'd just as soon not give them superpowers again if we can help it."

She nodded in understanding. "You get settled in your apartment?"

He shrugged one shoulder. "Yeah. It's all right. Ashley said I might get a roommate soon, at least for a while. Not too excited about that."

"I think we may have fixed that problem. We're working on a new building for recruits."

"Good. No one wants to live with me anyhow."

She could see how that might be the case. He wasn't exactly the most pleasant person she'd ever met. Yet, she also wondered if he'd ever remarry. He looked different in the tight black T-shirt he was wearing, as opposed to the fur coat he'd had on while he was a human in Russia.

"What?" He dropped his eyes to his arm, where she'd been staring, and Jo felt her face heating.

"Nothing. Just… no coat today?"

"It's eighty-five fucking degrees." His eyebrows practically touched. "You feeling okay?"

"Not really," she admitted. She definitely didn't want to admit she'd been checking out his biceps.

Ryker shook his head. "See you, McReynolds." He walked past her, and Jo continued on her way to the office.

When she walked in, she heard Jamie and Ashley's voices coming from the room in the back where they'd all met earlier. A few newcomers sat outside of Jamie's office where she could hear Cale talking in his grouchy voice. She continued down the hallway where she heard whistling coming from behind Christian's door.

With a deep breath, Jo considered knocking. Instead, she moved past his office to the former conference room. Maybe her mom and Elliott were right, and putting Christian in charge of anything was a bad move.

Or maybe Christian Henry was the key to saving the world from evil.

She wasn't sure she wanted to find out at all, but she knew for sure she wouldn't be discovering the answer right then.

6

Cadon

THE PIZZA PARLOR that had opened a few days earlier in the basement of the apartment complex mostly reserved for new recruits was hopping as Cadon walked in and looked around. Despite all of the people, mostly ones he didn't recognize, occupying nearly every table, it only took him a second to spot his friends. Scott lifted a hand, and Cadon waved back, making his way past the long line of people waiting to pick up their take-out orders to join them.

"There he is," Mandy said with her signature eye roll. "We thought maybe you weren't coming."

"Sorry. I had to have an uncomfortable conversation with my mom, sister, and your dad."

Mandy made a face. "Why is my dad at your place all the time? I don't think I've seen him for more than five minutes this week."

Shrugging, Cadon slid into the booth next to Scott, who scooted over closer to Leo Acres. Leo's sister, Fiona, was also there. "I think your dad missed my mom a lot for one," he replied. "And I think he misses my dad even more and is trying to convince us to open the Blue Moon Portal."

"Not a good idea," Leo said, plucking his beer off the table and taking a swig. "The last thing we need is to let someone like Holland back out of hell."

"I know." Cadon let out a sigh. "They say they just want to talk to him, but I'm not so sure."

"Not worth the risk." Fiona's voice was much quieter than her brother's, but her sentiment spoke loudly enough.

"I think my mom is going to do whatever she wants, and there's not much anyone can do to stop it." Cadon flagged down a waitress who started to blow him off, but once their eyes met, she smiled and headed over. He tried not to be irritated that his name made a difference here. "Can I get a Coors, please?"

"Sure thing, Mr. McReynolds," she replied with a wide grin. She was cute, but not his type with her wavy blonde hair. Lately, he'd been more into brunettes....

"It's Cadon," he corrected the girl before she headed off with a nod. "Did you guys order pizza already?"

"We were waiting for you," Mandy said with a shrug.

"When she brings you your beer, maybe we can order then," Scott proposed. "She seemed to like you."

Shaking his head, Cadon said, "I'll order the pizza, but I'm not into the waitress. Is she a human?"

"Yeah, most of the people who work here are," Leo explained. "It gives them an opportunity to stay in our safe zone and not have to worry about the Vamps."

That made sense. He hadn't been up to date on the nitty gritty since he got back from Alcatraz. "What do y'all want?"

"Pepperoni," Leo and Fiona said at the same time.

"With mushrooms," Mandy chimed in. Scott gagged. "On half!"

"Scott?" Cadon could see the waitress on her way back with his beer.

"Canadian bacon?" the Healer said.

"Okay, I think I've got it." The waitress set his beer down, and

Cadon said, "Can we get a large pepperoni, and a large half pepperoni with mushrooms and half Canadian bacon?"

"Sure thing, Cadon." The lights overhead gleamed off her teeth. "Anything else?"

"Cheese sticks." Mandy pointed a finger at the waitress for emphasis. "With marinara."

The girl nodded. "Is that all?"

"Yep, and a pitcher of beer when you get a chance. Thanks." Cadon forced a smile as the waitress nodded and walked away.

The conversation quickly shifted to when they might go on their next hunt if Cadence and Elliott were insistent on sticking around for the blue moon, but Cadon was suddenly distracted. Even though the parlor was loud and full of people, the moment Mallory walked through the door, his head whipped in that direction, as if he were drawn to her.

She didn't see him, though. She wove through the crowd of people standing around talking and got in line at the pick-up counter. Cadon bit his bottom lip, wondering if he should get up and go talk to her or just pretend like he didn't see her. Her dark hair looked glossy in the dim ceiling lights, and as she fidgeted with the sleeves of her jacket, he pictured the expression she was making, despite not being able to see her face.

"Earth to Cadon?" Mandy waved her hand in front of his face. "You in there?"

"Huh?" He quickly swiveled his face back to the table. "Oh, yeah. Sorry. I was just... wondering if the waitress was going to get that order right without writing it down."

"For the mighty Cadon McReynolds? Of course she'll get it right," Leo said sarcastically.

Scott turned and looked over his shoulder, probably just looking to see if the waitress had made it back to the kitchen, but then he saw Mallory, and a crooked grin spread across his face. "Oooh."

"Stop," Cadon insisted. "She's just a friend, that's all."

"Oh, is Mallory here?" Mandy pushed herself up off the seat. "She is! We should invite her over. She can sit by you, Cadon."

"Knock it off." Cadon took a sip of his beer. "She's probably picking up dinner for her mom. No need to–"

"Mallory!" Mandy stood and waved her arms, and Cadon sank down into his seat as far as he could. "Hey, Mal!"

Cadon took a deep breath and looked in Mallory's direction, trying not to seem mortified. Her lavender eyes were wide as she turned around.

"Oh, hi, Mandy. How are you?" Mallory asked before her eyes flickered to Cadon.

"We're good. You wanna join us?" Mandy gestured at the table.

"No, thank you," Mallory said quickly. "I'm picking up my mom's order, and I've got to get to bed soon. Early training, and I'm still not used to being up all night like you guys." An uncomfortable giggle slipped from between her lips.

"I'll see you in the morning," Cadon said dismissively and also giving her permission to ignore his boisterously loud friends.

"Take the pizza back to your mom and then come hang out with us," Mandy insisted. "We want to get to know you better."

Mallory's eyebrows raised, and her lips parted in an uncomfortable look Cadon knew well from pushing her at the gym. He started to tell Mandy to knock it off through the IAC, but then, he realized Mallory was saying, "Sure, okay. I guess I could for a little while."

"Yay!" Mandy literally clapped before sitting back down with a satisfied smile. "Cheers to another girl!"

Fiona chuckled and took a sip of her soda. Cadon could understand why Mandy felt like she was really the only girl around when Fiona rarely spoke, but he wasn't sure this was a good idea.

"It had to be rough," Leo was saying. "Living in a prison cell for the better part of her life, being terrified that she was going to be killed or turned into a Vampire at any moment. Damn, that girl's gotta be stronger than she looks."

"You can say that again," Scott agreed. "I don't think I could've handled it."

Cadon arched one eyebrow and considered what they were saying. He'd always seen Mallory as the timid girl he'd rescued during the Alcatraz mission, but they weren't wrong in commenting about how strong she had to be. It took a special kind of person to make it through the turmoil of being in that place for so long.

"It's too bad Hannah's not here," Mandy continued.

Confused, Cadon asked, "Why is that?" He knew Hannah was able to control people's emotions and thought maybe Mandy was saying she would be able to help Mallory feel calmer now that she was here, but he didn't really think that was a problem.

"Because she's a therapist, duh," Mandy replied, rolling her eyes into the back of her head and sticking out her tongue. "She could really help her. I still don't understand how she could just disappear. If President Crimson had executed the second in command of LIGHTS, wouldn't he have made a big deal out of it?"

"I don't think it makes any sense either," Scott agreed. "Besides, I was talking to this guy, Julian, who was one of the guys in DC. He says that his cell was right across from Hannah's. According to him, she was there one minute and gone the next, and he never heard her cell door open."

Now, Cadon was tuned in. "What? How is that possible?"

"I don't know, man," Scott said. "I was talking to him this afternoon at the gym, and he says he thinks something weird happened with her. He heard her talking to someone, and then she was gone."

"Talking to someone?" Cadon sat up straighter in the booth. "Who?"

"He didn't recognize the voice. You or Jo should probably talk to him. We need to figure out if Hannah is still alive." Scott picked up his beer and took a swig, and Cadon nodded in agreement. Something was off about the entire situation, and Hannah was too important to LIGHTS to just leave it be.

Mandy started a discussion about some of the new recruits that Cadon was only half-tuned into until the familiar scent of strawberry shampoo wafted his way. He looked up to see Mallory had returned. Mandy jumped up and hugged her and insisted there was more room on Cadon's side of the round booth, so Mallory brushed her hair back over her ear and slid in beside him. They were a bit cramped with her included, and her leg was pressed up against his.

Cadon slid a bit closer to Scott, but his friend wasn't budging, even though there was room on his other side. Cadon glared at the Healer, but he only smirked in response.

"Okay, here are those pizzas," the waitress said, setting them down, "and the cheese sticks." She'd dropped the beer off earlier. "Can I get you anything else? Another plate, I see." She narrowed her eyes slightly in Mallory's direction, which made the new Hunter flinch slightly.

Cadon wondered if it was because Mal was sitting so close to him. The waitress had been flirting earlier, after all. "Actually, Mallory wasn't here when we ordered. Is this okay?"

Her eyes flickered over the selection before she leaned in close to Cadon's ear. "I don't eat meat. I can eat the cheese sticks."

He had no idea she was a vegetarian. How had he missed that? A thousand questions flooded his mind. Had she been that way in prison? But then, he had no idea what the prisoners had survived on anyway. Maybe it was just gruel. Or rice. "Do you want me to order you a cheese pizza? I don't mind."

Her lips moved for a second without a sound coming out. He knew her well enough to understand what that meant.

"Can we get a small cheese as well?" he asked the waitress.

Her smile was back, even if it did look a little fake this time. "Of course, Cadon. Anything for you." She hustled off as Mallory made a grunting noise in the back of her throat.

Well, this is interesting.

"Do you mind if we dig in?" Scott asked Mallory. "I'm starving."

"Go ahead." She smiled at him, and Cadon offered her the cheese sticks and his plate. "Before Mandy eats them all."

"Can you blame me? I am my father's daughter." That got a laugh out of everyone.

The conversation quickly moved to normal young adult topics— like television shows and music—and no one asked Mallory about her time in prison, which he appreciated. It was nice, having her so close and not having to bark at her about doing more pushups or jumping higher.

About an hour after her pizza had arrived, she motioned to the waitress for the check. "I have to go."

"I'll get it," Cadon assured her.

"I can pay my part," Mallory insisted.

"I know you can," he began, even though he wasn't sure how true that was. Her mother had been in prison until recently, and he wasn't sure if anyone was getting paid again yet. "But I want to."

She grinned at him, and it was worth every penny. "I'll see you in the morning." Mallory patted his leg and slid out of the booth, leaving him staring after her.

"Walk her home, dumbass," Scott said, poking him in the ribs with his elbow.

Cadon turned to look at his friend, still in a daze. By the time his words registered and he realized he'd missed an opportunity, Mallory was gone.

7

Jo

AFTER A COUPLE of hours of shooting the shit with Jamie and Ashley, as well as a few other people who wandered into the conference room, Jo finally decided it was time for her to poop or get off the pot. As much as she didn't want to talk to Christian–at all, ever–she'd come over to the office building to approach the insane Revolutionary War general. So, she might as well see what the asshole had to say.

Excusing herself from the discussion going on with the others, which was back to whether or not they should be harboring Vampires, something she was tired of talking about anyway, she said she was heading home. Instead, she slipped down the hallway to Christian's office and quietly knocked on the door.

No one answered, and she didn't hear the sound of his stupid pirate song echoing through the hall, so she wondered if maybe he'd gone home for the evening. "Damn," she muttered, though part of her was happy she wouldn't have to speak to him.

Through the glass in the door, she saw the image from his giant computer monitor reflecting off the window behind it and could make out part of what he'd been working on. The image was familiar to her. Despite it being all black, she could see that he was looking at pictures from the tunnels of the Blood Moon Portal. But why? She had no idea. Could it be possible her mother had spoken to him about Jo's hair-brained plan?

Without thinking, she pushed the door open and stepped inside. The scent of cigarette smoke lingered in the air, but it was stale, telling her Christian had been here recently, but he wasn't here now. She walked over to the computer and bent down.

The image was of the tunnels, all right. She glanced down at a notation he'd made on a sticky note pad. "What the... 38.8977 N, 77.0365 W?" she read.

"Hey! You might think you're the boss around here, Little Mac, but I'll have you know, I don't take kindly to people nosing around my personal space." Christian barged in front of her, swiped up the notepad, and set a steaming cup of coffee down next to his computer.

"Sorry." She almost meant it. "I was looking for you and saw the reflection of your computer screen in the glass of the window. Why are you looking at the tunnels? We're done there—aren't we?"

"Yeah, of course we are." He dropped the notepad in his desk drawer and pulled his chair out abruptly, ramming it into her knee. Jo winced and stepped back. As soon as he sat down, he clicked over to a GIF of a cat playing the piano. "Now, all I have to do with my time is learn about the musical talents of tabby cats."

Jo narrowed her eyes at him. "I actually came to ask you a pretty important question, despite everyone I mentioned it to reminding me that you are the biggest asshole any of us have ever met, so maybe I should just leave you the hell alone."

She started to turn to leave, but he grasped her wrist, preventing her from doing so. "What?"

Jo spun back to look at him before wrenching her arm away. "It doesn't matter. It's stupid. And you can't be trusted."

Christian smirked, folded his arms, and leaned back in his chair so that the front wheel was off the floor. "I have no doubt it's stupid, if it's coming from you, and you're right, I can't be trusted. But if you've put enough thought into it to come all the way over here to ask me, well, you may as well spit it out."

Glaring at him, Jo considered whether or not to humor him. Part of her wanted to tip his chair over and laugh at him when he hit the floor, but the other part wanted to prove that her question wasn't stupid. With her anger about to boil over, she blurted, "Would it be possible to use the Blood Moon Portal to stop anything from coming back to earth from hell if the Blue Moon Portal opens?"

Christian's face went ashen as he dropped the front half of his chair onto the floor. "She's going to do it?"

Vague as the question was, Jo knew exactly what he was asking and nodded. "I don't think he'll come back but–"

"Son of a bitch!" Christian jumped up, turned around, and swiped all of the files off the desk behind him, along with a paper weight, a container of pens and pencils, and a framed picture that landed at her feet. Bending down to pick it up, Jo realized it was a picture of her mother which creeped her out immediately. "Mother fucker!" he shouted.

"All right. I think we're done here." She started to set the picture down on Christian's desk, but the photo of Cadence slid slightly, and she saw another photograph behind it.

This one was older. Curious, despite his reaction at her last bit of snooping, Jo moved the picture of Cadence and looked behind it.

The image was a daguerreotype of a beautiful woman with long dark hair dressed in western clothes.

Christian snatched the photo frame away from her and quickly placed Cadence's picture back in front of the other one. "Don't touch my shit."

"You don't think it's a little insane that you have a framed picture of my mother sitting on your desk?" she asked, whirling to face him.

"No, not at all. She's my friend, my only friend, as you well know, and I spent the better part of the last decade looking for her, so why would it be fucking weird for me to have her picture sitting here?"

"Because we found her!" Jo spat. "She's over there, in her apartment, with her real friends, trying to decide what the hell to say to my dad when she sees him again for a few days." She ran her hand through her short black and blue hair accidentally pulling out a few strands. "You are a fucking stalker."

Christian moved so fast, Jo barely had a chance to react. He hemmed her in against the desk, his eyes turning into squinting black lines. "Your father never deserved her. For over a century, all I ever heard was how fucking amazing Aaron McReynolds was. He's so fucking handsome, and so goddamn smart, and his farts smell like Drakkar Noir!"

"What?" Certain he'd lost his mind, Jo tried to push him back to get away, but he wouldn't budge. "You're not even speaking English!"

"I did everything I could to get her away from him, but she wouldn't listen!" His eyes went wide as he tossed his head back, his glossy dark hair catching the fluorescent lights above them. "Now that he's dead, she can finally get on with her life."

"Get the fuck away from me." Jo pushed him again, this time pressing both hands against his shoulders. He barely budged, and he probably wouldn't have moved at all if he hadn't wanted to, but it was enough room for her to squeeze out. "You are absolutely insane. I'm going to transfer you to... fucking Siberia or something."

"You can try to send me wherever the hell you want to, but I'll just open a portal and come back. You can't stop me from going anywhere, and you can't control me, so don't fucking try. You are not the Guardian Leader, and even if you were, I wouldn't give a shit. I do what I want to do, Josephine, and don't you ever fucking forget it." He folded his arms across his chest and narrowed his eyes again, and for a moment, Jo thought maybe she was facing one of those monsters he'd been so quick to kill in the tunnels.

Maybe he knew them so well because he was one of them.

"You're a psychopath." She started backing toward the door, wishing she never would've come there in the first place. One of these days, she was going to remember that the older members of her team knew what they were talking about, and she'd do well to listen to them.

As she reached for the door handle, he began to laugh. She turned and glared right back at him before spitting out, "I know what you do with a drunken sailor. You lure them into the fucking Blood Moon tunnels, kill them, and stack their bodies next to dead presidents. Earlie in the morning."

With that, she flung the door open and headed out into the hallway. She'd only made it a few steps before he shouted, "Alexander Hamilton was never president, you fucking moron!"

Jo made it a few more steps but didn't make it out of the building before the door to Jamie's office opened, and Cale stepped out. "What the fuck is going on?"

Groaning, she shook her head. "I idiotically went into Christian's office to ask him a question."

For the first time in a long time, a small smile parted his lips. "I guess you've learned your lesson."

"Yeah. Sorry for disturbing you. Do you still have patients?" She looked around, but the hallway was empty.

Cale shook his head. "No, the last one went to their new apartment about an hour ago. I've just been reviewing their records, trying to get an idea of what, if anything, the last few years have done to our DNA."

Jo's forehead furrowed. "You think this batch will be different than us?"

He shrugged. "I don't think so, but that side of things has always fascinated me."

Nodding, she leaned against the wall. Jo didn't know that much about Cale, only that he'd been some kind of area leader out in the west before she was born and had also run a medical practice that treated humans at one point. "You seem upset recently. Is everything okay?"

The physician cleared his throat and dropped his head. "I'm fine, thanks. Just… trying to get back in the swing of it all."

Once again, her head rocked back and forth, but she didn't believe him. Something was bothering him, and he didn't want to talk about it. "Well, if you ever wanna chat, you know where to find me." She forced a smile and headed toward the door.

Cale didn't respond, which she took as a sign that now was not that time. Jo stepped out into the fresh air and headed home, that ear worm about the stupid sailors replaying in her mind so that when she got to the elevator, she had to remind herself not to start humming it. Yet another reason to lock Christian Henry in the tunnels.

When she reached the penthouse, she unlocked the door with her IAC and walked inside to find her mother and Elliott sitting on the couch with a bottle of wine, laughing. She tried not to roll her eyes. She knew they had a lot of catching up to do, but why did he have to be here all the time? Sometimes she caught herself wanting to shout at him, "You're not my real dad!"

Jo managed to tell them both hello before heading to her room. She'd only taken a few steps before her mom's hand reached out and caught her wrist. "Why do you smell like cigarette smoke?"

8

Cadon

THE SOUND of his mother's voice hit his ear as Cadon lingered by the door to their apartment. He paused for a moment, reveling in the sound of it. How long had he been waiting to hear her soothing tone? The realization that she was actually home sank into his heart, but it was met with the memory that his father was not on the other side of the door, and that warm feeling quickly faded.

It didn't help that his mother sounded angry at the moment.

Cadon pushed the door open and walked inside.

"No, I didn't go there to talk to him," Jo was saying, her tone completely defensive. "I just happened to run into him."

"And did you mention your hair-brained idea about the Blood Moon Portals?" Elliott folded his arms across his massive chest and stared at Jo like he wanted to snap her in half.

"No, not really." Jo took a step backward, toward the hallway where her bedroom was located, like she was trying to escape.

Rather than interject himself into the conversation, Cadon continued to stand by the door, trying to decipher what they were arguing about based on the context. He had an idea Jo had told Christian her idea about him manning the tunnels to prevent anything evil from escaping, and both Elliott and their mom seemed super pissed about it.

"Jo, I told you that was a bad idea." Cadence sounded exasperated. "We have no idea what he is capable of."

"I understand that, Mom, but what I don't understand is why you continue to keep him around. Why is he here if he's so fucking dangerous?" Jo folded her arms right back in a stance of defiance.

"Because the asshole is like a cockroach," Elliott explained. "He won't die and he won't go away."

Sighing, Cadence brushed her hand through her hair. "He's left before. Nothing good ever comes of it."

"Jackass gets himself stuck in a hole in the ground again, I am not going to save him," Elliott muttered. Cadon felt like he should know what he was talking about, but he wasn't sure.

"We'll just have to make sure he's occupied that night." Cadence shook her head and turned to stare at Elliott.

"If he can fuck it up, he will." Elliott snarled, picked up his beer, finished it, and crumpled the can.

"Sorry. I guess I was just under the impression that I was in charge here–since I am fucking in charge here," Jo said with the same snarky attitude. "He's not going to do anything. He did have a whole lot of horrible things to say about Dad, though. I wanted to punch him in the face." Those were fighting words to Cadon. He perked up, ready to ask what the major might've dared say about the former Guardian Leader. But his sister didn't give him a chance. "And don't you think it's creepy that he has a picture of you next to his computer?"

Cadence turned to look at her daughter again, her eyes wide. "Still?"

Jo nodded. "Yeah, with some other woman's photo underneath. She was wearing western clothes."

"Brandy," Elliott mumbled, standing to walk to the kitchen, likely to get another beer. He took his can with him. "Woman doesn't know what she escaped in death."

"What?" Jo asked, but no one answered her.

"Just leave him alone, please, honey." Cadence reached over and took Jo's arm. "You seriously don't know what you're dealing with with him." Then she turned to look at Cadon. "You, too, sweetie. Stay away from Christian as much as you can."

Jo spun around to look at him as if she didn't know he'd entered the room, though he knew she had to have realized he was there. She didn't say anything directly to him, only glared at him before telling their mom, "I'm going to spend the night at Zane's." She rushed off toward the back bedroom, probably to pack a bag. At least he wouldn't have to listen to them making those awful noises all night tonight.

Cadon walked over and sat on the smaller of the two sofas, avoiding the uncomfortable chair. "What was that all about?"

His mom shook her head. Elliott walked back in and sunk into the couch beside her, saying, "Jo saw some images of the tunnels on Christian's computer and mentioned her idea to him. At least, that's what we gathered."

"And you really think that's a problem?" Cadon steepled his hands in front of his face, his elbows resting on his knees.

Before she answered, Cadence made a little noise in the back of her throat, one she must've made a hundred times a day since she'd been back. Realizing he was sitting just like his father, and that was traumatic for her, Cadon adjusted. "Yeah, it could be. We just don't know what Christian might do."

"How could he make things worse? It's not like he can do anything to hurt Dad now, right?" Cadon asked.

"True, but Christian is a loose cannon. He's unpredictable," Cadence replied.

"He's a fucking nut-job." Elliott cracked open his beer and took a long sip.

Jo came rushing back through. "See ya." She tossed her bag over her shoulder and pulled the door open.

Cadon couldn't see her, but the yelp of surprise she made had his head spinning. "Sorry."

"I'm sorry." Mallory's voice hit his ear, and Cadon practically leaped to his feet. "Is Cadon here?"

Rather than answering, Jo gestured in his direction and then brushed past the girl who'd apparently been about to knock on their door.

Hearing Elliott start that low rumbling laugh in the back of his throat, Cadon hurried over to the door. "Mallory? What's up?" He ushered her into the hallway before Elliott could say something to embarrass him.

"Sorry to bother you so late." She rubbed her hands together, looking up at him through her eyelashes. "My mom just got an IAC message from Christian. He said he's ready to do my IAC now. When Mom said that she would rather wait until tomorrow, he said now or never, so… could you go with me?"

Cadon's eyebrows furrowed. "Yeah, sure." He didn't mind going with her at all, but what did Christian mean by now or never?

"Thank you. Mom wanted to come, but she's tired. She's not used to working out so much." Mallory gave him an apologetic smile.

"It's no problem." The two of them walked to the elevator, and he wondered why her mom would be tired from working out because, as a Hunter, she shouldn't tire so easily, but she had spent many years in a prison cell. Maybe that had something to do with it.

The elevator ride down seemed longer than normal, and they spent most of it in silence. Cadon commented on the electronic version of a song he sort of recognized playing over the speakers, but Mallory didn't respond.

She really was a woman of a few words.

They arrived in the lobby and made their way over to Christian's office. In light of the discussion he'd just heard, nerves bubbled up inside of him. If he had to defend Mallory against the craziest person he'd ever met outside of a blood-thirsty Vampire, he would do so, but he'd just as soon not have to get into a brawl with the weird fucker if he could avoid it.

When they reached the door to the office, Mallory slid her hand around his arm. "It'll be fine," he told her. She nodded, but he recognized the frightened look in her eyes. Unfortunately, he'd seen it too many times.

By the time they reached Christian's office, the grip on his arm had increased so that he was pretty sure his fingers were no longer getting any blood. He kept his concerns to himself and knocked on the door.

It flew open hard enough to hit the wall and bounce off, making Mallory jump. "Enter." Christian had a cigarette hanging between his lips. He darted off toward the back of the office.

Waving his hand through the smoke, Cadon entered the office. The only light illuminating the large, messy space was the glow from the massive monitor sitting on Christian's desk. As they passed by, he noticed the picture of his mother sitting there and cringed a little.

In the back of his office, Christian had a large chair he used for "patients" getting their IAC implanted. It was the same one that had been there when Cadon was younger and had his put in. He remembered there being a bit of pain with the procedure, but it was nothing like the Transformation process, and he'd been told it was also likely because of his bloodline that it hurt so much–same as Transforming.

So when Mallory asked, "Will this hurt?" he was fully prepared to say, "No."

But Christian beat him to it. "Probably." He pulled the cigarette from his lips and dropped it in an overflowing ashtray. "Sit." He stood in front of his desk, fiddling with something. Cadon couldn't see it in the dim light, but he assumed it was her IAC.

Mallory did not get in the chair. Instead, she looked up at Cadon, her eyes wide with worry.

"It'll be fine," he assured her. "But if you want, I can get Scott over here, just in case."

"Not waiting for Scott." Christian plunked down on a rolling stool. "I've got forty more of these to do tonight, so let's get a move on."

"Why are you in such a fucking hurry?" Cadon asked, glaring at him.

Narrowing his dark eyes, Christian said, "Because I am leaving soon, but I have to get all this shit done first."

"Leaving?" The conversation he'd heard earlier came back to him. "Where are you going?"

"To Noneofyourfuckingbusiness," Christian snarled. "Ever heard of it? I bet you have. You're your father's son, you know it? But last I checked, I don't answer to you."

Remembering what his sister had said about Christian bad mouthing his dad, Cadon was ready to launch himself across the chair and punch Christian in the face. Only Mallory gripping his arm kept him planted. "Well, since my mom and sister know nothing about it, and you do answer to them, maybe you should let someone know."

Christian grumbled under his breath, but all Cadon could make out was something about, "Won't miss me anyway," and he had to imagine Christian was talking about Cadence.

In his mind, he sent a quick IAC message to Cale, Scott, and Jamie, the three Healers he could think of off the top of his head, and then turned to Mallory. Flashing her the most relaxed smile he could muster, he said, "It'll be fine. It really doesn't hurt."

"Are you sure? He said it does, and he's the one that does them." Her bottom lip quivered a little.

"Pansy," Christian mumbled.

"I'm sure–" Cadon began, but before he could finish, the office door opened, and Cale walked in. "Besides, now Dr. Ryan is here, so if it does hurt, he can help you." Through the IAC, Cadon let Scott and Jamie know they were no longer worried.

"Someone's getting her IAC, huh?" Cale's tone was more relaxed and kinder than it had been for as long as Cadon could remember. "Don't worry. It won't hurt." He smiled reassuringly at Mallory. "Christian just likes to scare people. But if it does sting a little, I can take care of it."

"Let's get on with it." Christian gestured to the chair.

Swallowing hard, Mallory had a seat, sliding her fingers down Cadon's arm to grasp his fingers. He gave her hand a reassuring squeeze.

Christian walked through the process–how he'd put some

numbing drops in her head, make a small incision, and then insert the IAC. He'd give her some antibiotic drops to take a couple of times a day until it healed, which shouldn't take long. She nodded, and Christian placed the drops in her left eye. Her right eye stayed focused on Cadon's face.

A few moments later, Christian picked up the scalpel, and Mallory flinched. "I can restrain your head if I need to," he threatened.

"It'll be okay. Just look at me." Cadon smiled wider.

Mallory nodded and took a deep breath. This time, when Christian moved in, she didn't budge.

But she did whimper a little and bit down on her bottom lip. Cadon just kept smiling. Once Christian dropped the IAC in, he slid away from her. "Done and done."

Sitting up, Mallory blinked a few times. "That's it?"

"That's it. Told you it wouldn't hurt." Cadon helped her up, thinking she might be a little dizzy. She latched back onto his arm. "I'll teach you how to use it tomorrow, okay?"

"Thank you." She gave Cadon a thankful smile.

"You're welcome," Christian barked, sarcastically.

Mallory turned to him. "No, thank you, too. I do appreciate it."

"Whatever. Get out of my office so I can get the next set of eyeballs in here."

As Mallory thanked Cale, Cadon couldn't help but lean down next to Christian's ear and whisper, "I bet Brandy thought you were just as much a psychopath as the rest of us."

Growling, Christian turned, his hand already in a fist. Cadon was faster, though, and caught it before he could make contact with his face. "Get the fuck out of my office now, McReynolds, or you won't have to wait for a blue moon to see your father."

"What's happening?" Mallory asked as Cale also questioned the situation.

"I'm not afraid of you, Christian," Cadon said, still meeting his gaze. "I'm leaving to walk Mallory home, but trust me, if you and I meet again, I'll make you wish you'd never said anything bad about my dad."

"Just remember, little boy, I still have a whole cabinet full of titanium bullets."

"All right, let's break it up." Cale stepped between them. "Really, Christian, shave already. You look like Captain Caveman. Let's go."

The Healer ushered Cadon and Mallory out of the office as Christian began to whistle that fucking pirate song.

9

Jo

ZANE'S FINGERTIPS dug into her hips as Jo rode him, her head tossed back as she concentrated on the euphoria building inside of her. He grunted a few times, letting her know he was close, but she silently begged him not to come first. She needed this—after the day she'd had, boy did she fucking need this.

As if sensing her irritation, Zane reached between her folds and brushed his finger over her most sensitive area. That was exactly the trick she needed. With him prodding her along, she finally fell over the cliff, letting out a loud moan as she spasmed around him. Moments later, he followed, and she dismounted, tossing herself onto the mattress beside him, panting and covered in sweat.

"Well, hello to you, too," he muttered, taking the condom off and tossing it into the trash can next to his bed. "I take it everything isn't peachy keen in the McReynolds-Sanderson household for you to knock on my door and then assault me?"

A chuckle escaped Jo's lips as she wiped perspiration on the back of her arm. "Sorry. No, things are not all peachy keen, and it is not the

McReynolds-Sanderson household. He just won't ever fucking leave." She'd met him at the door and practically tackled him, dragging him into the bedroom without so much as a greeting.

With all the tension gone, or at least most of it, Jo pulled on the T-shirt she'd been wearing, which she found at the foot of the bed. Zane's eyes followed her every move. "What's going on?" he finally asked.

She shook her head. "Nothing. I just... I asked Christian what he thought about trying to prevent something coming through from hell by monitoring the Blood Moon tunnels. He freaked out, and when Mom found out, so did she. And Elliott." She tried to shrug it off but couldn't.

Once she was resituated, lying next to him, Zane reached over and took her hand. "Did you tell them you asked him?"

"Not at first. Mom smelled the cigarette smoke on me and knew." She really wished that imbecile didn't have to smoke so fucking much.

"Well, if your father doesn't come through the portal, it won't matter," Zane reminded her, pulling her over to lie against his chest. Her head nestled right over his heart, which was still pounding loudly.

"I know." It was all she could think to say. Deep down, she understood the chances of Aaron coming back through the portal were slim, but she had to hope that he would—and that they'd manage to prevent anything dangerous from coming through with him.

"Try to get some sleep." Zane kissed the top of her head.

"You, too." She knew he didn't need sleep like she did, but he'd lay there with her until she passed out and then untangle himself and go do something else. In the morning, he'd be there with his arms wrapped around her. There was comfort in that.

The next day, Jo decided she needed to go have a talk with Christian. If he had it in his head to do something dangerous, she needed to talk him out of it.

She walked into his office, ready to give him a piece of her mind, but he wasn't there. That stale smell of smoke lingered in the air, not the fresh stench that often told her he was hiding in the back some-where. Nor did she hear that ridiculous song.

"Christian?" she called, spinning around. "Are you here?"

No answer.

She was just about to use her IAC to try to locate him when Jamie's voice had her spinning toward the door. "He's gone."

Eyes wide, Jo asked, "What do you mean?" Had he gone to get more coffee? Out for breakfast? For a walk?

Shrugging, the Healer walked toward her. "He told me late last night, after he finished putting in the rest of the IACs we had lined up that he was leaving. When Ashley asked him where he was going, he told her it was none of her fucking business. I told him not to let the door hit him in the ass."

It was clear Jamie was irritated at his fellow Guardian speaking to his wife that way. "So you think he *left* left? As in… he's no longer on the campus?"

"That's the impression I got. He was carrying a backpack, and he didn't have his IAC on. It's still not on."

"Seriously?" Jo leaned back against Christian's desk. "Where in the world would he have gone?"

"I don't know," he admitted. "And I kind of don't care."

She could agree with him on that. Still, it seemed like not knowing where Christian was might make the situation even more dangerous as the blue moon grew closer by the moment. "We should probably try to find him," she muttered. "Can mom force his IAC back on?"

Jamie shook his head. "No, no one can. Not even your dad."

"What?" Jo didn't know anyone else had an IAC that worked that way—other than her mom—and that had been some sort of fluke, as far as she knew.

"He designed them and made sure that he had total control over his," Jamie explained. "Look, Jo, I know he's a nut, but he's probably just pissed that your mom hasn't given up on your dad and wants to speak to him. Christian probably thought that he could find a way to make her take notice of him and potentially use her grief to ingratiate himself to her."

It was difficult for Jo to hear. The idea that Christian, who'd said such awful things about her father just the day before, might be able to weasel his way into her mother's life made her angry in a way she couldn't put into words. "I just hope he's gone for good."

"I wouldn't hold my breath," Jamie murmured, taking a few steps toward the door. "We'll need to find someone else to put in the IACs while he's gone."

Jo turned toward Christian's desk and noticed the photo of her mother—and Brandy, whoever the hell she was—no longer sat next to his computer. Had Christian taken it with him?

"Jo?"

Jamie's voice had her turning her head in his direction. She processed what he'd just said. "Right. Is that something Emma can do?"

"I'm not sure. She's got the tech side down, but actually cutting into someone's eye? I don't know." Jamie shook his head.

"Maybe it'll be a two person operation from now on? Do we have plenty of them made?" She had no idea how her parents had been in charge of LIGHTS for so long. Just a few months of being the boss, and she was overwhelmed.

"We should have several hundred, but I'll check on it." He gave her a meager smile that was meant to be reassuring and sympathetic, she thought.

"Thank you, Jamie." She meant it. He was one of the most important team members for sure, one she could absolutely rely on.

"Sure thing. I'd better get back to my office."

She heard him open the door, but distraction had her delaying her response again. She'd pulled open Christian's desk and noticed his note with that latitude and longitude written on it was gone. What could that mean? "Damn." She slammed the drawer closed.

"Something wrong?" Jamie asked, pausing in the doorway.

"Yeah. I'd seen a note Christian had scribbled down on a notepad. It looked like a lat/long. I have no idea if it was important or not, but he didn't seem to like me looking at it," she explained.

Jamie's forehead crinkled. "With him, it could be anything. Do you remember what the numbers were?"

Jo took a deep breath and blew it out, cursing herself for not having taken an IAC image of the note. She shook her head. "I had just picked it up when he walked in. The first number was 38 something, and the second one was 77."

"Hmm." Jamie folded his arms and leaned back against the doorframe. "Could you tell how old it was?"

She shook her head. "No. But it was on the top of his sticky pad."

"Christian hasn't been in the office much in the last decade, so that doesn't mean anything," he pointed out.

"True." Jo scanned the office. She didn't notice anything else missing, but she did see a camera up in the corner of the room. The red light was off, indicating it was no longer in use. "Too bad that thing isn't working."

"The camera?" Jamie stepped back into the room. "It probably is."

"The light's not on," she pointed out.

"Yeah, but ever since Christian lied to your parents about the Retransformation serum being ready when it wasn't, which almost killed your dad before you were even born, I'm pretty sure it's always on."

"Where would the feed be recorded?" she asked, wondering if she could pull it up on her IAC or Christian's computer.

Without replying verbally, Jamie walked over to Christian's computer and moved the mouse to turn on the monitor. He logged Christian out and logged in himself. A few clicks later, he pulled up an image from the camera that appeared to be off. Jo watched herself rocking back and forth nervously in real time until Jamie backed the video up.

Soon enough, they were looking at an image of Christian standing where they now stood from the early hours of the morning. He reached into his desk, pulled out the notepad, yanked the top sticky off, scrunched it up and shoved it in his pocket. He never turned it so that Jo could see the writing on the feed.

Then, he took the picture off his desk and shoved it in his backpack before turning toward the camera and flipping it off.

"So he knew he was being recorded," Jo noted.

"Wait...." Jamie cautioned.

Christian typed a few commands into the computer and then turned back to look at the camera, laughing.

"He thinks he turned it off?" Jo asked.

"Looks like it."

"Dumbass," she muttered.

But then she watched in horror as he did the one thing she needed him not to do.

Christian opened a portal and stepped through it. Through the rippling edges, she could see inside. The sight of familiar black tunnels had her heart sinking in her chest.

10

Cadon

"But what if I accidentally send someone a message I don't mean to?" Mallory asked. She wrapped her fingers around the edge of the bench in the gym where she sat next to Cadon, frustration showing on her beautiful face.

"You won't." He'd already assured her for the twentieth time, but it was clear she still didn't trust him. "You can't send anything without using the commands I've told you to."

She shook her head, her soft brunette curls dancing around her shoulders. "I don't think I can get used to this."

"You will. You should just practice. Maybe only send messages to your mom for a while." They'd finished their workout about an hour before and agreed to meet back here to work on her IAC training. Cadon had rushed through the shower, but it had taken Mallory forever to reappear. At least Christian hadn't been in the men's locker room.

She took a deep breath and let it out slowly. "I don't know. I feel like–"

Before she could finish the sentence, Jo's voice flooded his mind as an IAC message came across, one that seemed so important, he wasn't able to pay attention to both of them at the same time, and his mind chose Jo's unbelievable message. *"Christian's in the tunnels."*

"Cadon?" Mallory said. The feel of her hand on his arm had him tuning back into her. "Did you hear me?"

"I'm so sorry, Mal. I didn't. My sister just sent me an important message."

She pulled her hand away, immediately leaving him cold. "I thought you were supposed to be able to pay attention to the IAC and whoever was talking to you at the same time."

"I usually can," he said with a shrug. "But this was really important. We have a bit of a problem. Can we practice this some more tomorrow?"

He saw her shoulders relax. "Yeah, of course." She was clearly glad that she wouldn't have to keep trying to get the device in her eye to work. "Is everything okay?"

Somehow, Cadon managed a nod. "Yeah, everything's fine." That wasn't true, but there was no reason to alarm her. It's not like she could do anything to help him anyway. "I need to head home, though."

"I'll walk with you." She stood, grabbing her bag, and he tried to be happy to have a few more moments with her, but she wasn't as fast as he was, and he'd have to walk slower than he otherwise would have so that she could keep up.

Fresh air hit his face as they walked outside. Lots of people he didn't recognize strolled around the compound. Most of them looked a little lost and nervous. Ordinarily, Cadon would slow down to help them, but not today, not with the news Jo had just sent him. He'd let her know he was on his way to the penthouse.

"Is it about the next mission?" Mallory still sounded a bit nervous as she hurried alongside him. Cadon made a conscious effort to slow his steps. "Have the Vampires attacked again?"

"No, it's nothing like that," he replied, shoving his hands into the pockets of his jeans. "It's just Christian. He's gone somewhere, and we need to find him."

"Why?" She ran a hand through her hair. "Isn't it just as well that he's gone?"

"It would be, but we think he might be back in the tunnels, and he really doesn't need to be messing around in there," he explained. He saw no reason to tell her the rest of the facts.

"Well, I hope he doesn't cause any trouble." She smiled up at him, and Cadon felt reassured that everything would be okay.

"Thanks. Me, too."

They arrived at the apartment building and headed for the elevators. It seemed to take forever for one to arrive. Cadon took some deep breaths, trying to stay calm. He couldn't do anything about finding Christian at the moment anyway. He really wished his sister hadn't said anything to Christian about the stupid fucking tunnels.

Inside of the elevator, Mallory used her finger to press the button. "You could do that with your IAC," he reminded her.

"Or I could accidentally send the entire elevator plummeting to the basement, killing us both." She shrugged her shoulders and pursed her lips together.

"Well, that wouldn't kill you now." Relief that she wasn't as vulnerable as she had been when they first met washed over him.

"True." The elevator stopped, and the doors opened. "See you later, Cadon."

"Bye, Mal." Once she was out of the elevator, he took another deep breath, wishing he could've spent more time with her and been more straightforward, but he knew it was difficult being a leader, knowing specific information everyone else wasn't privy to, and keeping it to himself.

A few moments later, he arrived at the top floor and rushed across the hall to the penthouse. Voices filtered through the closed door, letting him know several people had gathered inside.

"We don't even know why he went in there," his mother was saying as Cadon walked in and closed the door behind him.

"Well, it can't be for anything good," Elliott replied from where he paced in front of the fireplace.

Jo, who stood in front of the window across from Elliott, next to

Zane, had her arms folded across her chest in a way that made Cadon assume she already knew this was her fault.

Jamie, Ashley, Scott, Cassidy, and Brandon also filled the space which was beginning to seem small to Cadon for the first time.

Afraid to ask the wrong question and end up getting himself into trouble, Cadon took the only available seat–the uncomfortable chair–and sucked it up.

"We need to figure out how to open a portal so we can see what the hell he's up to," Cassidy said. She sat next to her sister on the couch, her legs crossed, her foot swinging back and forth rapidly.

"No one else knows how to open it," Jamie reminded her. He was sitting on the armrest of the smaller couch, across from Cassidy, next to his wife and son.

"Do you think there's information on his computer? Maybe we can get Emma to hack into his files and find something," Jo suggested. "If Christian can figure out how to open a portal, Cassidy has to be strong enough to do it, too."

"I don't think I can do that," Cassidy admitted, shaking her head.

"Maybe he's actually trying to do what we asked him to do," Cadence said, though her tone conveyed that even she didn't believe it.

"Nope." Elliott shut her down. "There's no way."

"What could he possibly do from inside the tunnels that could mess with the Blue Moon Portal?" Cadence argued back. "We don't even know for sure that you can reach hell from the portal, and you certainly can't reach 'the beyond.'"

"We don't know any of that," Cassidy replied. "We didn't think there were layers to hell, but it turns out that there are. Christian spent the better part of ten years in there. He could be up to something so devious we'd never be able to figure it out."

"Or he could've just decided that if he couldn't be with Cadence, he may as well go back to where he's the most comfortable. He likes killing the monsters in there. Maybe that's where he feels most like he did when he was a cowboy in the old west." Brandon's point seemed to resonate with everyone but his father.

"He'll find a way to make a catastrophe happen." Elliott stopped his pacing and turned to look in Brandon's direction.

"We should probably just wait until he gets back before we open the portal." Cadon's mom sighed and brushed her hair over her shoulder. "It's the only way to be safe."

"Or… we can alert the rest of the LIGHTS teams around the world about what Christian is up to and have them all on high alert, especially in the places where we know the Blood Moon Portal opens," Cassidy offered. "As long as Aaron doesn't try to come through the Blue Moon Portal, it shouldn't matter. Christian won't be able to unleash anything evil into the world."

"You're probably right," Cadence agreed. "I just hate going through with it when Christian may be up to something."

Elliott growled and rammed his fist into his palm. "So fucking stupid."

"I'm sorry, okay?" Jo pushed off the wall. "You guys never should've let me stay in charge once Mom got back."

"It's not your fault, honey," Cadence argued as Jo walked toward the hallway that led to her room. "It's not easy being a leader. I know I struggled with it for years."

Jo paused next to her mother. "I resign. Cadon… you're in."

"Wh–what?" His mouth hung open as his sister disappeared. Zane patted his shoulder before following behind her. Everyone else in the room turned to look at him. "Why would I be in charge?" He turned to his mom. "You've been back a while now. Don't you think–"

Cadence gave him a reassuring smile. "She's just upset. She'll be okay in a day or two."

"We only have a few days," Elliott reminded them. "The blue moon will be happening before we know it. Of course, Christian would find a way to fuck this up."

Cadon didn't hesitate to say, "I don't want to be in charge, Mom. I had enough of that when I was at Alcatraz."

"You did a great job at Alcatraz," Jamie reassured him. Everyone who was there–Brandon, Cassidy, even Elliott–nodded in agreement.

Shaking his head, Cadon said, "I don't care. If it hadn't been for

Heather, and the rest of you, we would've gotten annihilated." He thought about how difficult it was to get Mallory out of there unscathed, let alone everyone else.

"For now, I think we should continue to plan to open the portal, just to talk to Aaron," Cassidy said, putting her hand on her big sister's leg. "We'll take every precaution to make sure nothing bad happens, and you know he won't come through."

Cadon watched the color drain from his mother's face. "I don't know."

"I know." Cassidy patted her knee. "He won't come through, so it doesn't matter. You'll just get to tell him you love him, and he'll know you're safe."

"He doesn't even remember we exist right now," Jamie reminded all of them.

"Knowing Aaron, he does," Elliott replied. "I didn't remember anything, but he will."

"Just in case," Cassidy continued. "We will reassure him, and then you'll get to tell him goodbye–for now. He won't come through. And no one goes in." Cassidy looked at all of them, but her eyes lingered on her sister's face.

"Of course, no one goes in," Cadence agreed. "There's no way in hell anyone is going in."

"Good," Cassidy said. "Let's get a plan in place to mitigate Christian's potential damages, and move forward as planned."

Cadon nodded in agreement, thankful that he'd get to say goodbye to his father, but also glad that Cassidy seemed to be in charge.

Anyone but him.

11

Jo

STEPPING down from her position as leader hadn't quite gone as planned. A few days after she'd stormed to her room, with the blue moon looming just three days away, Jo made her way to Christian's office with a cup of coffee in her hand, wishing she had more time to run and less shit to worry about.

Her IAC went off several times during the short walk, alarming her of situations across the globe where newly emerging members of LIGHTS stormed into Vampire strong-holdings, taking out as many as they could. Several governments, including the United States leaders, were still in hiding.

It might've seemed like those were more pressing issues than figuring out what the hell Christian was up to, but Jo couldn't let it go. If there was a chance at all that he could fuck up her mother getting to say goodbye to her father, she had to prevent it from happening.

And that meant getting inside the damn portal.

In Christian's office, Emma Burk and Lucy O'Sullivan, two of her aunt's closest friends, sat behind keyboards, typing away. Emma was on Christian's computer, using his massive monitor, while Lucy had a laptop and sat on the other side of his desk.

"How's it going today?" Jo asked. Jamie had gotten the two of them started on trying to figure out how to open the portal the day after they'd had their meeting about Christian disappearing, but so far, they hadn't discovered anything.

"It's slow going," Emma said, adjusting her glasses. She didn't need them since she'd Transformed, but she'd decided to continue to wear them because it was what she was used to. Jo didn't know either woman well, but she'd come to understand Emma, the more techy of the two, was a bit unusual. Lucy, on the other hand, was a fashionista with perfect hair and acrylic nails that Jo thought should make it impossible to type.

"Emma's crawling through the camera footage, and I'm still looking through everything on his IAC," Lucy explained. "We thought we had something for a minute, but it didn't pan out."

"What was it?" Jo asked, stifling a sigh of frustration.

"He had some kind of device on his wrist, and we thought maybe that's what he was using to open the portals, but he didn't use it that way. At least, not in anything we've found yet." Emma adjusted her glasses, pushing them back up her nose.

Folding her arms, Jo leaned against the desk. "When we were in the tunnels, he sort of waved his hand. Zane asked him how he opened the portal, and he said, 'Science.'" The memory had just come back to her. "Maybe he did have some sort of wristband that did something."

"When the portal originally opened, the weirdo doctor who was working with Holland used mirrors and onyx," Lucy explained. "Is it possible Christian found a way to capture that in a wristband?"

"But that only worked during the actual blood moon," Emma pointed out. "Why would it work any other time?"

"Maybe he found a way to replicate what happened during the original blood moon and reproduced it in some kind of device." Lucy moved her head to the side a bit so that she could see Emma.

Blowing out a long breath that blew her brunette bangs around, Emma leaned her head on her hand, her elbow on Christian's desk. "I don't know. I guess it's possible."

"My dad would've had to have one, too," Jo reminded them. "He was also able to open the portals." The two exchanged another glance, but Jo wasn't sure what it meant. "If we can figure out how he did it, we'd have to make another one."

"Unless...." Lucy stood up, tapping her finger against her chin. "Where's your dad's stuff?"

"Huh?" Jo's forehead scrunched. "What stuff?"

"The stuff he had on when he... died," she clarified. "Maybe he was wearing it."

Jo continued to stare at her for a long moment. It couldn't really be that simple, could it? Had her dad had on anything other than the watch he always wore? She couldn't remember. "I'll have to ask Elliott."

Both of the girls nodded, and Jo stood up, taking a few steps away from them, still a bit dazed thinking about where her father's personal effects might've gone to.

"We'll keep looking," Lucy promised her as Jo turned and walked to the door.

"Thanks."

On her way back to the apartment building, where she was fairly certain she could find her uncle since he never seemed to leave the penthouse unless he was going on a food run, she was lost in her own thoughts and almost ran into Ryker–again.

"Sorry," she muttered, trying to step around him.

"Jo?" He moved to block her again. "What's going on?"

"Nothing. I just have a lot on my mind." She ran her hand through her hair, accidentally pulling out a few blue strands. "Do you need something?"

"I'm just wondering... I heard that you wanted to send Christian and some other members into the tunnels again the night of the blue moon."

She nodded. "That's right. But he's gone."

"Right." He took a deep breath and folded his arms, his biceps bulging under the tight gray shirt he wore. Jo told herself not to notice, but it was difficult not to. "I don't like this. I think he's up to something."

"We're trying to get in there now to see what he's doing," she assured him. "I'll keep you posted."

"Please do." He dragged a hand down his face. "If it smells like shit, it's usually shit."

Not knowing what else to say, she nodded again and stepped around him. This time, he didn't move to block her.

A few moments later, she walked into the penthouse apartment to find Elliott eating Cap'n Crunch out of a mixing bowl. He grabbed the remote and flicked the television off, but not before Jo recognized he'd been watching that weird show from the 1980s with the four old ladies.

Shaking her head at his life choices, she asked, "Where's Mom?"

"Out working on something with Ashley." He brought the tablespoon to his mouth, milk and a few yellow pieces of cereal tumbling back into the container. He only half-chewed it all before asking, "What's up?"

Sighing, she said, "I need Dad's stuff."

Elliott's forehead crinkled. "What stuff?"

"The stuff he had on when he… died." It was still hard to say the word.

He set his bowl aside, something she'd rarely seen him do. "Why?"

"Emma and Lucy think Christian might've created some sort of a device to open the portals," she explained in a rush, not really wanting to get into all of it but knowing she'd have to in order to get what she needed. "If Christian had one, Dad must've had one, too."

He began to shake his head before she even got the sentence out. "Nah, he didn't have anything like that."

"Are you sure?" Exasperation filled her body as she folded her arms. "You didn't burn everything he had on him, did you?"

Narrowing his eyes, Elliott stood. "No. You know I didn't burn his wedding ring. Do you think I'd burn his watch?" He shook his head as he strolled toward her mother's bedroom. "Give me a little bit of credit, Jo."

Everything had happened so fast after her father died, Jo hadn't asked a lot of questions. They'd been in a foreign country. Holland was gone. They needed to get home so she could begin to search for her mother. She wasn't sure what all had happened. She'd been wearing her father's wedding ring on her thumb for a while, but she'd given that to her mother.

Opening Cadence's closet, Elliott walked in and began to survey the shelves. They were fairly empty compared to how they had been before the Revelation. A few of her mother's outfits hung on one side. The other was empty.

Visions of how the closet used to be filled with her parents' things, her father's button-down shirts and slacks, his leather jackets, all of that, came back to her.

In the back of the closet, Elliott reached up and pulled down a box that was larger than Jo was expecting. She didn't step over to see what all was in it, afraid she might see Aaron's bloodied shirt or something, but she caught a flash of black leather and knew his favorite jacket was in there. She looked away. She'd had no idea Elliott had also taken a box from the funeral home when she carried out Aaron's ashes.

Elliott stepped over toward her a few moments later. "Just his watch, and his jacket. His ring is in here now, too."

She turned toward him and nodded. In his extended palm, he held the ring and the watch.

"Mom knows this is here?" She picked up the ring first and held it for a moment, refusing to let tears fill her eyes. She'd forced herself to wear it in the portals, but it was still hard to look at.

"Yes," he assured her. "She said she might let your brother have the ring one day."

Not knowing how to respond to that, she set it back in Elliott's large hand and picked up her dad's watch.

He always wore it, even though he had the time in his eye. For as long as she could remember, it had been this Rolex, too. The time was still set correctly; it hadn't been that long since he died.

Not long enough to have to replace the battery.

It looked like a regular watch, but she couldn't know for sure if Christian had modified it. He, too, always wore a watch after all. A vision of him checking the time when he didn't need to raise his wrist to do so came to mind.

"Can I take it in for Emma and Lucy to look at?"

Elliott shrugged. "Sure. Just make sure they don't do anything to tear it up. I'm sure your mom will want to keep it."

"We'll be careful. Thanks."

He nodded and turned to put the ring back in the box.

Taking a deep breath, Jo started to walk out of the room, but movement outside caught her eye. Pausing, she stared out the window.

The fountain. It was completely restored.

She knew Juan Diego had been intending to work on it. He'd told her as much a few days ago. But she hadn't realized he'd done it.

Elliott's huge palm came down on her shoulder. "It's beautiful, isn't it?"

All she could do was nod.

"I commissioned it. Your dad loved it. Before you, that was the closest thing to a little girl he had."

Jo stared at the smiling stone face that was meant to represent her little sister, Aarolyn. When she was younger, she used to wonder what it would be like if her big sister had lived. Maybe she wouldn't have been such a wild child if she had an older sibling to give her advice—and take away some of the pressure of being the oldest McReynolds child.

Shaking her head, she pushed the thought aside. It didn't matter now. Aarolyn was dead, and their father was finally with her. "Thanks for your help," she muttered to Elliott, pulling away from him.

"Don't lose it," he yelled after her.

She raised a hand to let him know she'd heard him—again—and headed back to the offices with the watch in her hand.

Emma and Lucy were back to work, looking through the surveillance footage of Christian's office and searching his IAC. They both paused as soon as they saw her walk through the door. "All he had was his watch," she explained, extending it to Emma.

The girl took it, frowning. "That's too bad."

"Could it have been modified?" Lucy asked, walking around the desk. "Christian always wore a watch, too. I know that. I'm not sure if he had on anything else. He might've had a device that got covered up by his sleeve."

"It looks like a regular watch to me." Emma stood and took a few steps away, toward the wall. Jo wasn't sure what she was doing, but her eyes went to the frozen image of Christian sitting at his computer. What was that bastard up to?

"We probably need a back-up plan in case we don't figure this out in time." Lucy sounded as frustrated as Jo felt. She ran a hand through her long blonde hair. "God, he was such an asshole."

"He was," Jo agreed. "I don't know what else we can do, though. We've already alerted the teams around the world to be on high alert. We just have to be sure that no one comes through the Blue Moon Portal."

"I don't think there's any chance your father will come through," Lucy said. Jo met her blue eyes and nodded. "He always said he didn't want anyone to come through it."

"Yeah, I know. I'm just afraid something crazy is going to happen, that's all."

"Like what?"

She didn't get a chance to answer Lucy's question before they both heard Emma say, "Holy shit!"

Jo and Lucy both turned their attention to where Emma was standing. A black hole hung in the air in front of her, blocking the view to the wall. Jo's eyes bulged, and her mouth dropped open. "How did you do that?"

"The watch was modified," Emma explained, not turning to look at them. "That's it, right? The same kind of portal you went through to get to the tunnels?"

Jo didn't want to get any closer than she already was. "Yeah. Looks like it." She wasn't going in there.

Emma turned to look at them, continuing to hold the watch up so the portal stayed open. "Looks like we've solved one problem."

"Yeah, now we just need to–"

Lucy's statement was interrupted as the portal began to shimmer, and then, a human form tumbled onto the ground, landing at Emma's feet. All three girls gasped in surprise, and Emma let go of the button on the side of the watch, the portal closing.

Jo drew her weapon. "Who the fuck is that?"

12

Jo

With her Glock drawn, Jo stepped around the desk where Emma stood with her mouth held open. She had also drawn her gun, but now, the girl was gasping in surprise and shoving it back into its holster as she dropped to her knees. "Oh, my god!"

Unsure as to who the woman lying on the floor next to Emma's feet happened to be, Jo kept her gun drawn. A cascade of long strawberry-blonde hair hung over the woman's face, obscuring her identity.

Apparently, Lucy and Emma knew who she was despite not being able to see her face. "Are you okay?" Lucy asked, diving over to where Emma was now kneeling. "What the fuck?"

"I'm okay." The woman's voice was soft and calm, despite the fact that she appeared to be in rough shape. She was wearing dirty jeans and a gray T-shirt that appeared to be too big for her. Her bare feet left smears of blood on the floor where she'd stepped through the portal and continued to drip as she adjusted where she was sitting. If she'd been in the tunnels for long, with their black volcano rock-like flooring, bare feet could've easily been shredded. Jo reupholstered her weapon.

"We've been so worried about you." Lucy wrapped her arms around her. "Were you in there the whole time?"

The woman shook her head. "No, just a couple of years. Where the fuck is Christian?" The serene note to her voice changed slightly as she looked around the room. It was then that her eyes locked on Jo and a soft smile lit her face. "Hi."

Jo's eyebrows knit together as recognition slipped into place. "Hannah?"

She nodded. "That's me. How are you, Jo?"

"Uhm, I'm fine, but… what the fuck?"

It was the question of the day. "It's a long story. Is Christian here? We're in his office, right?"

"We are, but no, he's not," Emma answered, matter-of-factly.

Lucy let Hannah go and stood, offering her hand. "I'm calling for Jamie on the IAC. Your feet look awful."

"I'm sure that's not all that looks awful," Hannah mumbled as she got up. "Jamie's here? He's okay?"

Lucy led Hannah to the chair she'd just been sitting in. "Yes. We killed Holland and freed the prisoners in Washington and Alcatraz," she explained. "I don't know what all you know."

Hannah sat down with a sigh of relief. "Thank goodness. Is everyone okay?"

"Not everyone," Emma replied. "Aaron died."

Hannah's eyes bulged, and Jo instinctively took a step back, like she should somehow escape the harshness of the response.

"Em!" Lucy nudged her in the arm. "Don't be so blunt."

"Sorry." Emma shrugged like she didn't understand what she'd done wrong.

Hannah's eyes fell on Jo's face again. "Oh, my. I am so sorry."

"Thank you. I know he loved you very much." She wasn't sure what else to say.

Before Hannah could respond, Jamie came flying through the door. "Oh, my god!"

A smile lit Hannah's face as she stood up. Jamie wrapped her in a hug. "I'm so glad to see you."

As soon as she touched him, her feet stopped bleeding. Jo had seen it a million times, but it still astounded her just how quickly he could heal anything.

If he got there in time....

A moment later, a rush of LIGHTS members flooded the room. Jo backed up, letting them in. Everyone rushed over to hug the Guardian, some of them crying. A dozen voices asked where she'd been, how she got there, and a thousand other questions, but Hannah didn't get a chance to answer before someone else would come in to hug her.

When Cadence walked in, Hannah's mouth dropped open, and her face paled. It was about the same reaction Emma and Lucy had had when they realized who'd just fallen through the portal. "You are alive," Hannah whispered. "And you're back."

Cadence crossed the room, and everyone parted to let her through. She hugged her friend tightly. "I'm so glad you're okay."

"It's amazing to see you," Hannah replied. "And I'm so sorry about Aaron."

Tears glistened in her mother's eyes as she said, "Thank you. He thought the world of you."

"Hannah, where the hell have you been?" Elliott demanded, making his way through the crowd to stand right next to Cadence.

Taking a deep breath, Hannah said, "I was trapped in a strange layer of tunnels underneath the Blood Moon Portal tunnels," she explained.

Cadence gasped. "Me, too. Did Holland's minions put you there?" Her mom still didn't talk a lot about what had happened after she'd been kidnapped by the Vampires, but she had confirmed she'd been taken to the Blood Moon Portals by Holland's Vampires, and then Holland had taken her to that special tunnel of torture somehow. It was something she'd created inside of the portal in all the years she'd been there.

"No." Hannah's eyes narrowed to slits. "Christian did."

The room went silent. Mouths dropped open, and a few people looked around the room as if they were expecting the missing Guardian to suddenly appear and answer their questions.

"Wh-what?" Cadence's question finally broke the silence. "Christian put you in a tunnel like the one I was trapped in?"

Hannah's head rocked back and forth. "At first, I thought we just got separated. He showed up in my cell in DC one day and asked me to come with him. Of course, I didn't hesitate. I was just glad to be out of prison. He told me he was helping Aaron look for you." Her eyes met Jo's mother's, and a nod passed between them. "He showed me this set of tunnels beneath the original tunnels, but I wasn't looking when he accessed them because he had me watching for monsters. We just seemed to fall through the floor, and then we were in a similar place, but it was definitely different. A weird white light kept glowing in the distance. We followed that, and I ended up all alone."

Jo knew exactly what she meant by the same but different. A shiver went down her spine as she thought about how hopeless she'd felt running around down there in those tunnels.

"Did he just ditch you?" Lucy asked, shaking her head.

"At first, I thought it was an accident, that he just couldn't hear me, but then I couldn't find him, and then he turned off his IAC. I couldn't even follow him to try to track him." Hannah took a deep breath. "I don't know how long I was in there. It seemed like a couple of days or maybe a couple of centuries. I finally managed to find my way out of the white space back into the faux tunnels, and then I searched and searched for the way out. When I finally realized I was going to have to propel my way through the ceiling to get out, it took me a long time to find a way to do that."

"How did you manage?" Jamie asked, probably remembering his own stint in the portals.

Hannah took a deep breath and brushed her hair out of her face. It was full of black ash, and her face was streaked with it as well. That spark of kindness Jo remembered always seeing in her eyes was long gone and replaced by the solemnity only betrayal from a trusted ally could create. "I started killing monsters, dragging their bodies over, and stacking them up."

Jo's eyes widened in astonishment. "I don't think we saw any monsters in those fake tunnels."

"No, there weren't a lot of them," Hannah said. "Not compared to the ones in the real tunnels. But there were some. Eventually, I was able to get out, but the first several times I tried to go through a portal when it opened, nothing happened."

"When was that?" Cadence asked, holding her breath.

Jo understood why and waited for the response.

"Not long ago, I don't think. I just managed to get back to the real tunnels recently. Time is so different in there, it's hard to tell, and the clock in my IAC is all screwed up. When I saw this portal open, I was on the other side of the tunnel, but I made a run for it." Tears filled Hannah's eyes. "I can't believe I'm back here."

"You're here now." Cadence pulled her friend against her shoulder. "You're safe."

"We should get you something to eat, a shower, and some clean clothes." Ashley stepped through the crowd to join Hannah and Cadence. "I'm sure you're exhausted."

"We have a lot of questions," Emma blurted out. "When did Christian take you from Washington, DC?"

"Uhm, I'm not sure." Hannah wrapped her arms around Ashley and Cadence for support. "I can go back and check my IAC."

"Let's let her rest, and then we'll get it all sorted out." Cadence used her free hand to pat Emma on the shoulder. The tech girl nodded and moved away from the touch.

When Hannah left, the crowd cleared out, leaving Emma, Lucy, and Jo staring at the wall where the portal had opened–and Aaron's watch.

"So Christian didn't change anything about the rules," Lucy said, shaking her head. "The only reason you were able to get your mom out is because Hannah was in there. You still have to leave someone behind. All this time, Christian knew that, and he lied to us about it."

"What a shocker," Jo replied in a sarcastic tone.

"Well, the good news is, now that Hannah has found her way out, Christian won't be able to leave." Emma's face took on a morbid smile.

"That's true!" Lucy grinned right back at her. "Give the bastard a taste of his own medicine."

While Jo understood their point, the situation made her nervous. Knowing Christian, he had other tricks up his sleeve. Still, this solved their problem for now. They wouldn't have to worry about Christian causing shenanigans during the blue moon if he was trapped in the portals.

Reaching out a hand for her father's watch, Jo said, "I'll take that for safe-keeping."

"You just push these two buttons at the same time to open the portal," Emma said, but she didn't touch them.

"I don't think we'll be going back in there any time soon," Jo told them. They both laughed, but she had a feeling she was just kidding herself.

13

Cadon

CADENCE HAD SELECTED a clearing in the woods behind the LIGHTS campus as the place where they'd try to make contact with Aaron that night. Reluctantly, Cadon walked along behind his mother, sister, Elliott, Jamie, Hannah, Cassidy, Brandon, and Zane wondering how this was all going to go down. He had a bad feeling in the pit of his stomach, regardless of the fact that Christian was, apparently, locked in the portals.

"We have about ten more minutes," Elliott announced. He was wearing a backpack he refused to explain to anyone, and the smirk on his face seemed to scream that he was up to something. Surely, he wasn't going to try to convince Cadon's dad to come back, was he?

Cadence carried the urn from the fireplace, but Cadon still thought it smelled suspiciously like it was filled with ash out of a barbecue pit. All of this was confusing, and while he did want to see his father and have a chance to tell him goodbye, he also hoped it would all be over soon.

He also wished that Mallory were with him. Seeing Jo and Zane holding hands made him miss her even more. But the contingency was already massive, and he couldn't think of a simple explanation to invite her along, so he stood in the back by himself wondering if the damn portal would even open.

Elliott spoke about setting the ashes up like he was an expert. "You want to make sure you get the full effect of the moon." He looked around. "We might be too close to the trees."

"The trees are behind us." Cadence elbowed him and stepped forward into the clearing, still holding the urn. "I'm the one that's done this before."

"Well, we were in a desert," Elliott reminded her. "The trees are behind us, but if the moon comes up that way…." He lifted an arm and ran a trajectory across the sky. "I think we should scoot forward a bit."

As Elliott and Cadence continued to bicker, the group spread out a bit. Cassidy and Brandon hung over to one side, like they were there more as emotional support to Cadence than to actually see Aaron, which made sense to him since Cass was his mother's sister. They'd been close to Aaron, of course, but they knew their place.

So did Zane. When Jo took a few steps in Cadon's general direction, he hugged the perimeter, doing his best to stay out of the way.

Shaking her head, his sister said, "What do you think about all of this?"

Cadon opened his mouth, closed it, and then finally said, "I don't know what to think. Do we even know how long this thing will be open?"

"Mom says it's like five minutes, ten tops," she said with a shrug. "I'm not sure she knows, though. It was a long time ago when she brought Elliott back."

"Does it have to be right overhead, or can it be at an angle?" Cadon looked over at the moon as it began to climb across the sky. It would be another hour or so before it was straight above them.

"Who knows?" Jo let out a sigh and turned around so she could see the bickering friends. "Do you know what you're going to say to him?"

Tears welled up, blocking Cadon's ability to say anything at all for a moment. "There's a lot I'd like to say," he finally managed. "But I'm not sure I need to say it in front of everyone and their uncle." His eyes turned to Brandon. He'd been considering "and their boyfriend" but he didn't feel like jabbing his sister at the moment.

She nodded. "Same. I'd like to think he can hear me when I'm whispering my apologies late at night, but both Mom and Elliott say they don't remember us at all."

"Maybe it's more like a sense of peace they can feel when we apologize," Cadon offered. "Instead of actually hearing the words."

"Maybe." Jo didn't seem to accept that. She cursed under her breath and lifted her face to the sky. "I just want to get it over with."

"Same." Sometimes saying less was saying more.

"Shouldn't be long now," Elliott said, once they had the urn in place. He slipped one massive arm out of the backpack and swung it around in front of him so he could unzip it. Tugging it open, he dug inside and pulled out a large Ziploc bag–full of ashes.

"Are you shitting me?" Cadence exclaimed, shoving him. "I knew it!"

"Well, I couldn't take any chances on Christian doing something," Elliott explained. He moved over to the urn and dumped it out. "Smells like hot dogs." He laughed and looked at Cadon who could only shake his head.

"I swear to god that man has lost all his marbles." Jo swore under her breath again and headed over to stand next to Zane. Cadon preferred to hang back. As far as he could tell, the Blue Moon Portal wasn't doing anything yet, so there was no reason to stand there and stare at nothing.

The minutes ticked by slowly. Cadon wandered around, occasionally tuning into the various conversations happening amidst the other group members, but he never said a word to anyone. At one point, he thought he heard something moving in the trees behind them, but he didn't see anything, and the idea of running off to investigate further and missing his father wasn't worth entertaining.

"Holy shit, here we go!"

Elliott's boisterous voice had Cadon turning back around to face the group. At first, he didn't see what all the commotion was about. Everything looked the same to him, but then he took a few steps closer and realized the air above his father's remains was shimmering slightly in a soft blue glow.

"Fuck," Jo murmured, stepping up to stand right next to their mom and Elliott. Cadence had her hands folded in front of her face, her bottom lip clamped tightly between her lips. Cadon took a spot right behind her, and when she glanced over her shoulder at him, he could see tears glistening in her eyes.

They stood there for a couple of minutes, watching the blue lights intensify before a familiar form began to appear amidst the glowing orbs. Cadon took a deep breath and watched as the swirling lights fell into place, and then, he was staring at his father.

Cast in a warm sapphire glow, Aaron squinted a few times, tilting his head from side to side and peering out at the gasping crowd. In front of him, Cadon heard his mother whimper and then start to cry.

"Cadence?" His tone conveyed confusion and recognition as he leaned forward but never left the safe space of the portal. "Is that you?"

"It's me." She took a few steps forward until she was only a foot or two away from her husband. Jamie went with her, keeping his arm around her waist as a reminder for her not to go in, Cadon assumed. He must've been the only one thinking about that because Cadon wanted to rush up and give his dad a hug.

"You're okay." It wasn't a question. Aaron let out a deep breath and smiled. "Thank goodness."

"Jo found me." Through her tears, Cadence managed to get out the words and tip her head back in Jo's direction.

Cadon's sister stepped forward. "Hi, Dad. We miss you."

"Jo. It's good to see you. But don't come any closer. Where's your brother?"

"I'm right here." Cadon felt like a little boy again, lunging forward to get his dad's attention. He stopped behind Jo. "I miss you so much."

Aaron's fond smile warmed Cadon's heart. "I'm so sorry I had to leave you guys. We didn't get to say goodbye."

"We don't have much time," Cadence blurted, finally realizing the truth of the situation. "Are you okay? Do you remember us?"

"I'm just fine," he assured them all, looking around the crowd. He acknowledged the others with a wave and a smile. "I honestly didn't remember, but that's okay. We'll all be together here one day. It really is beautiful."

Cadon noticed his mother lifting a hand to wipe away a tear. "We will be. And you're with Aarolyn and Aislyn now, so…"

"Yeah, I am." Aaron didn't say more, but then, what could he say? It had to be hard for him to talk about his first wife to his second one.

The blue lights began to shift, vibrating and getting closer to one another. Aaron's form wavered with the change in energy.

The portal was beginning to close.

"Any chance you wanna come back?" Elliott shouted.

"Elliott, no!" Cadence said, shaking her head. "We know you don't want to. You don't have to. It's okay. We can talk like this sometimes."

"I wish I could, but I can't risk it." Aaron's voice broke a bit with the statement, and next to him, Cadon felt Jamie's muscles strain a bit as he tightened his grip on Cadence. "Holland's dead. The world should be better. Let's not mess that up."

"We don't want to do anything dangerous," Cadence said.

"Hannah, it's good to see you're home. Everyone, thank you for coming to say hello." Aaron began to ripple again, and the lights around the perimeter of the circle grew even closer together. It was going to be impossible to see him in a moment. Caden was glad he'd turned his IAC on to record earlier so that he'd at least be able to see his dad again when this was all over. He didn't know when the next blue moon was, but it was likely months away.

"I love you!" Cadence shouted as the portal got even smaller.

"I love you, too. So much." Aaron took a deep breath, the light around him growing dimmer. "I'll see you next time. I hope–"

Whatever he was going to say was cut off by a loud crashing sound behind him and the sound of panicked screams in the distance.

"What the fuck?" Aaron turned to look over his shoulder. "How the hell did those get in here?"

Frantic cries for help and what sounded like a large amount of people running, as well as roars and banshee-like screams filtered through the waning portal.

"What's going on?" Cadence tried to take another step forward, but Jamie pulled her back.

"I... I have to go. I don't know how, but there are monsters in here. I love you guys." Aaron shook his head and turned around, disappearing from sight, but the sounds of horror didn't stop.

"We have to get to the tunnels," Hannah whispered.

"No, we need to go through the Blue Moon Portal and help him!" Cadence shouted, trying to move forward again.

"We can't!" Jo stepped between her mother and what was left of the portal. "Mom–if we go through this way, we'll unleash Demonic Vampires in the world."

"We don't even know if the portals link!" Cadence frantically tried to break free, but Elliott and Hannah had her shoulders now. Cadon stood weighing his options. Should he bolt through the small remaining opening in the portal and help his dad?

"Fucking Christian!" Jo shouted. "Mom, please, don't try to go this way. We'll figure it out!"

Just as Jo finished her statement, a large black tentacle reached out of the remaining opening, which was only about a foot across at this point and wrapped itself around Jo's waist.

It all happened so quickly, Cadon didn't have time to respond. One moment, Jo was standing there pleading with her mother to let the portal close, and the next, she was almost folded in half as she was sucked through the fading blue lights. Then, she was gone!

Cadence screamed, and Cadon took a few steps forward. Zane lunged to follow her, but Brandon and Cassidy both grabbed him and pulled him back. They couldn't afford having two Demonic Vampires unleashed on the world.

In all the chaos, Cadon almost missed the dark streak that shot from the forest to the portal and dashed inside right as the blue lights faded and the portal was gone.

Almost.

14

Jo

Jo hit the ground hard with a thunk that jarred her jaw and had her eyes rolling back into her head. Looking up, she saw a crystal blue sky with white puffy clouds floating by, and no trace of any portal opening.

A slithering sound and the increase of pressure around her waist was a staunch reminder that she'd been tugged through the Blue Moon Portal by something.

Tipping her head back, she saw a set of razor sharp teeth coming at her and realized some large black octopus-like monster with the face of a tiger had grabbed her and pulled her through. Now, it seemed that fucker wanted to eat her.

As the teeth came flying down, she reached for her weapon and found out that she couldn't get to her gun. It was the only weapon she had with her, but the tentacle wrapped around her was keeping her from getting to it. Jo's only hope was that someone would come and help her before it was too late.

If she died here, would she just regenerate here? How did one die in the place people went when they were dead?

"Get off me, you fucking asshole!" she shouted, jamming her hands up in hopes of poking the sucker in the eye or something before it could bite her head off. Her hands slid up the slimy surface of the monster, but it was far stronger than her, and in a moment, it was all going to be over–whatever that meant.

The pinging sound of gunfire rang out from in front of her. Jo couldn't tip her head to see who was firing, but their aim was true, and the monster promptly fell backward onto the velvety green grass, its grip on her waist releasing as it dropped.

With a deep inhale, Jo wiped the slobber from her face and unwrapped the dead limb from around her in time to see an offered hand.

With her fingers firmly wrapped around her savior, Jo found herself being hoisted up off the ground. Her mouth dropped open in shock as she stared into a familiar face. "Ryker?"

"Are you okay?" he asked, shifting his Beretta on his shoulder.

"I'm fine. But what the fuck are you doing here? Did you get sucked in, too?" She spun around as he walked in the direction where the screaming and shouting was coming from.

"No, I followed you through," he admitted.

"What? Why?" Anger pulsed through her as she realized that meant two Demonic Vampires had just been unleashed on the world.

Ryker sighed in frustration, picking up his pace as more monsters became visible, chasing citizens down the street.

Jo took it all in. The picture in front of her seemed like something out of a Rockwell painting mixed with something out of Goya's worst nightmare. The little town could've been Mayberry, USA, with its cute little houses and shops, perfectly manicured lawns with trees and hedges trimmed and molded spectacularly, and no trash or dirt in sight. Conversely, a large number of the black monsters Jo was familiar with from the tunnels charged after the citizenry, their sharp teeth and claws reaching out to grab and maim.

Deciding she could shout at Ryker for breaking protocol again later, she pulled her Glock and shot a half-horse, half-walrus creature in the head right before it chomped down on a little boy. The child screeched and lunged for a woman who had to be his mother. She gave Jo a thankful look and ducked inside what appeared to be a grocery store.

But the people weren't safe inside either. A black snake with legs rammed its face against the window of a flower shop until the glass broke. It slithered inside, causing a fresh burst of screams from those who were attempting to hide in the building.

Working together, Jo and Ryker rushed the creature, with her grabbing hold of the tail and giving it a tight pull while he blasted it with his gun several times at an angle that wouldn't put the people inside at risk.

The snake reared its head, its long pink tongue lashing out as it turned toward Ryker. He took another shot, landing this one in its left eye, and the creature went down.

Pausing to catch her breath, Jo surveyed the chaos around here. She easily spotted another twenty to thirty monsters running down the road in front of her, and from the sound of it, the situation behind her was similar.

"Look at that shit!" Ryker pointed up at the sky where every few seconds a flash of light appeared. The bright beams shot down into the same field of grass where Jo had landed. "What the hell?"

"That's the dead folks regenerating."

Jo turned to see a woman with silvery-white hair wielding an ax standing next to her. The blade of the weapon was covered in ash. "Wh-what?"

"When you die here, you come back right here," she explained, her eyes locked on the sky as well. "'Course that doesn't happen very often since we usually have peace and happiness here." When the woman finally turned to look at her, her forehead furrowed. "My, you look like Cadence."

"Cadence?" Jo repeated. "You… you know my mother?"

The woman's face softened. "Oh, yes. You must be Jo."

Her eyes bulged. "How did you know?"

With a laugh that didn't quite fit the mayhem around them, she said, "Because I'm your great-grandmother. My name is Janette. Now, come along. Let's go kill some monsters and find your father."

Still not sure exactly how her great-grandmother, who had disappeared through the Blue Moon Portal before she was born, knew who she was, Jo decided that was a topic they could discuss later–like maybe after she died, if she made it out of here alive. She ran off after the woman who looked like she was sixty but ran like she was six. Was that a result of being dead or being a Hunter? She didn't know, and there was no time to find out.

"This sure is a fine mess!" a man who looked to be about the same age as Janette hollered to them as he shot at the monsters. "In all my years, I've never seen anything like this."

"I know, Jordan. This is insane," Janette agreed. "We have to figure out what happened and ensure it never happens again."

"I can tell you what fucking happened," Jo bit out, shooting a monkey-opossum in the side of the head. "Fucking Christian Henry happened."

The man turned and looked at her, his forehead creased. His eyes were very familiar, and she realized that was because they were her mother's eyes. Jordan–Great-Grandpa Jordan. "Christian?" he repeated. "How the–oh, you must be Jo!" He smiled. "It's lovely to meet you, dear, though not under these circumstances. You aren't dead are you?"

"No," she said, shooting some sort of a koala bear on steroids over his shoulder. "An octa-tiger pulled me through the portal."

He nodded and turned back around, shooting another monster without batting an eye, like he'd been doing it his whole life. But then, he had been the Guardian Leader for a really long time, hadn't he?

"We need to find Aaron," Janette said, tossing her ax at an oncoming monster. She lifted her hand, and another ax generated in her palm.

"How the fuck did you do that?" Ryker asked from over her shoulder.

"Language, children," Janette scolded. "We are in 'the beyond' where everything is supposed to be nice and pleasant."

"Sorry," Jo muttered, realizing she'd said a few swear words, too. "Can you just pluck whatever you want out of the air?"

"More or less," Janette said with a nod. "But you won't be able to." She looked at Jo and then at Ryker. "Neither of you belong here."

Jordan turned to give Ryker a suspicious look but then went back to killing monsters.

"We got big problems, Miss Janette." A kid who looked to be about sixteen ran out of a house off to the side, one already covered in ash from monsters climbing all over it. "People are dying and regenerating and then dying again." He brushed some ash off his dark skin and ducked as a large black bird swooped down at him. Jo didn't want to take the shot because she was afraid she'd miss and hit him, it was so close, but Janette threw another ax.

"Reggie, you're not trained to fight these monsters," she told him. "Go hunker down somewhere."

"But that's just it. They're everywhere. They keep pouring through." He pulled a gun from his waistband and shot at one of the monsters, but it took several shots to come anywhere close to hitting it, and then Ryker aimed and shot it between the eyes. Clearly, this kid wasn't a member of LIGHTS.

From behind him, another young man emerged. Jo blinked a few times, noting that this guy looked like a lanky version of Elliott. "They bit mom's leg. She's bleeding pretty bad. I managed to kill it."

"Oh, fiddle," Janette mumbled. "I'll go help. Jimmy, go back inside. You, too, Reggie." As she ran toward the house, Janette paused and looked at Jo. "You need to find a way to get back to your mama. I'm sure she's missing you."

Jo nodded. "I will." But—how? Wasn't the only way out of here through the portal? "Fuck," she whispered, looking down at her wrist. She wished she'd convinced her mother to let her wear her father's watch, but her wrist was bare. Still, it looked like her dad was wearing the same clothes he'd had on when he died. If he had it.... "Dad can close the hole Christian made with his watch."

"Are you sure that's what happened?" Ryker asked, rushing up beside her. "How do you know for sure that Christian did this, and how do you know it's a portal opening?"

"It's the only thing that makes sense," Jo replied as Jordan shot an elephant-sized monster that was bearing down on them. "We have to find my dad and make sure he doesn't close the portal before we can get on the other side." She looked at Ryker for a moment, meeting his gaze. "Unless...."

"Unless what?" He reached up and wiped his brow. Little dots of perspiration reclaimed his hairline immediately. Despite the perfect weather, he was sweating. It could've been exertion. Or maybe it was something else.

"Do you want to stay?" she asked, looking around. Most of the people who'd been fleeing from the monsters had made it inside, but she could see a few people scurrying down the streets or coming out of buildings and attempting to dodge back inside. For a moment, she was distracted by a woman who looked remarkably like Ashley, but it wasn't her. She refocused on Ryker. Was his family here somewhere?

He narrowed his eyes, that angry glare he almost always wore reclaiming his face. "I didn't come here to find Clair and the girls," he assured her. "I came here to help you."

"Okay." She took a deep breath. "But do you want to try to see them before you... leave?"

He shook his head. "No." His tone was full of resolve, but she had to wonder if he was just putting on a tough guy act. "We have to get through that portal before your dad closes it."

She nodded, deciding to let it go. He was a grown ass man, and he could make up his own damn mind. "All right. Let's go."

Before she could say another word, she heard a horrendous scream, and her attention was pulled off to the side. Between two houses, she saw a beautiful woman with long flowing red hair huddled over a baby as a huge monster loomed, ready to snap them both between its teeth.

"Oh, fuck," Jo muttered. "It's her."

15

Cadon

"Jo! Jo!" Cadence was beside herself, screaming at the darkness where the portal had been only moments ago. Everything had happened so quickly, Cadon barely had time to process it all. One moment, Jo had been there pleading with their mother not to try to go through the opening. The next moment, she had been gone.

"We'll have to find another way." Elliott had his arm around Cadence's shoulder, trying to console her, but it was clear she was terrified she'd never see her daughter again.

Cadon's heart broke for his mother. Sure, he'd miss his sister, too, but they'd never really gotten along. At the moment, he was more worried about his mother's condition. She'd finally made her way out of the tunnels only to learn her husband was dead, and now her daughter had been snatched from her by a monster.

"She's not alone in there." Cadon barely recognized his own voice as realization set in. Over the cacophony of everyone trying to reassure Cadence and come up with a plan, he wasn't sure anyone heard him.

No one addressed his statement, so he said it again, louder this time. "Hey, guys?" It was almost a shout. "She's not alone."

"We know." Jamie's voice sounded reasonable enough. "Your dad will keep her safe until we can figure out how to get her out."

"No, it's not that." Cadon remembered the feeling he'd had earlier that someone else was in the woods, how he'd thought he'd heard something, and he recalled the black streak that had disappeared through the opening as the portal was closing. "Someone else went in."

"What the fuck are you talking about?" Cassidy asked. "When?"

"Right before it closed," Cadon explained. "You all must have missed it, but I saw it."

"Someone else went in?" Zane's voice cracked a little as he spoke. "Someone else managed to follow my girlfriend in there when you guys wouldn't let me?"

"Are you sure?" Elliott asked, turning to look at Cadon over the tops of everyone else's heads. "With all those dancing blue lights, sometimes it's hard to see–"

"I'm sure." Cadon pulled up his IAC video and shared it with everyone, trimming it so that it started right after Jo disappeared. He saw no reason to make his mother relive that ordeal.

A hush fell over the crowd as they watched the film, and their mouths dropped open. "Who the fuck is that?" Cassidy asked.

Cadon slowed it down and watched it over and over again, but he wasn't sure. The shadowy figure moved so quickly, even in slow-mo, it was difficult to tell. It looked like a male....

"Ryker." Zane said the name like it was poison on his lips. "It was fucking Ryker."

Confusion swept over them as Cadon and the others tried to figure out what Zane had against Ryker, other than the fact that the bastard had taken matters into his own hands and Transformed in the tunnels without permission to do so. Cadon hadn't spent a lot of time with the guy. He mostly kept to himself and seemed like a good dude, but it was clear from the glare on Zane's face that he wasn't pleased.

"That means we now have two Demonic Vampires unleashed in

the world," Elliott pointed out. "Dammit. If we just could've talked Aaron into coming through, we'd only have one."

"And Christian would be terrorizing the people in the beyond without Aaron there to help undo whatever the hell he's doing," Cadence reminded them, wiping her eyes. "It's a good thing that Aaron didn't come back."

"I'll notify all of the teams around the world to be on the lookout for two Demonic Vampires," Jamie said, switching into catastrophe response mode. "We need to get Aaron's watch, get in the tunnels, and find Christian. Maybe we can force him to do whatever the hell he just did to let those monsters into 'the beyond,' and we can find a way to get Jo out."

"And Ryker," Hannah added.

Jamie shrugged. "Sure, if he wants out. Didn't his family get killed by Vampires or something? Maybe he doesn't want out."

Cadon wasn't familiar with Ryker's backstory at all, but at the moment, all he could think about was making his mom happy. She was supposed to gain closure from this event, not have her heart ripped out all over again. Stories about what went on in the tunnels made him cringe, but he knew he'd have to go in there.

"I'm pretty familiar with the tunnels now," Hannah said. "I can go back in."

"You should stay here and lead things." Cadence turned and looked at her friends. "It's too soon."

"I'm going." Zane's voice made it clear no one should argue with him, so no one did.

"Unfortunately, Brandon and I are pretty familiar with them, too," Elliott said, clapping his son on the shoulder.

"I did a lot of exploring through the tunnels that lead to hell," Cassidy chimed in. "I think Christian had to have made this hole to 'the beyond' down there somewhere, so I'll go, too."

"It's settled then. We know who's going and who's staying behind." Cadence rushed off ahead of the rest of them, leaving Cadon going over the conversation in his mind as he hurried to catch up to her.

Had they decided who was staying and who was going?

A few moments later, they reached the entryway to the apartment building. Cadence was already gone, clearly in a hurry to get to her daughter.

"Should we wait here or go up?" Elliott asked. "Surely, she'll want to open the portal in Christian's office and not in her own apartment."

"What difference does it make?" Cassidy asked, folding her arms.

The enormous Guardian shrugged. "I don't know that it does, but I'd rather we do it where Christian has always done it in the past. If he needs to use a portal to get back here, I think we should have some people waiting to take him into custody. That asshole has a lot to answer for."

"I can get a group together," Hannah said with a nod. She had more of a reason to want to punish the bastard than almost anyone else.

"You should probably ambush him in the hallway so he doesn't have a chance to pop back into the tunnels," Jamie suggested.

"Or shoot everyone." Cadon shook his head. He wouldn't put it past Christian to do that.

"We're going to need a Vampire to go with us." Brandon spoke up for the first time in a while. "We won't be able to get out of there if we can't leave someone behind."

"Fuck," Elliott muttered. "You're right. Cadence is in such a hurry to get in there and get out that she's not thinking straight."

"Why don't we set up a secondary team to bring in a Vampire to leave behind once we get in there?" Jamie suggested.

"How are they going to open the portal if we have the watch?" Cadon asked.

More swearing peppered the air as they all realized they had some details to work out.

The door to the apartment buildings opened, but it wasn't Cadence who walked out. Cadon hid his gasp as Mallory's violet eyes met his. A smile lit her beautiful face as she stepped over to him. "Hey, what's going on?" She glanced at the others, and her smile slowly faded. "Is everything okay?"

"No, my sister got sucked into the portal," he blurted. "We have to go get her."

Mallory's forehead wrinkled in confusion. "What? How?"

"Something reached out and grabbed her and sucked her in. We think Christian did something to mess with the portals so the monsters from the Blood Moon Portal got into 'the beyond,' the place where the Blue Moon Portal opens." It was a rush of words, full of terms she probably wouldn't understand.

Mallory nodded. "What can I do?"

Before he could answer, Cadon's mother came flying out the door behind where Mallory was standing, holding up the watch. "Let's go to Christian's office!"

"Nothing," he assured her as he fell into step with the others. Cadence was gone again, but he wasn't going to try to keep up with his mother. They still needed to make sure they had plenty of munitions and discuss the details.

"Where are you going?" Mallory reached out and grabbed his arm as she hurried to keep up with him.

Taking a deep breath, Cadon explained, "I'm going with the team to get her back."

"What?" Her grip on his arm increased. "What? No, you can't go in there. It's dangerous."

Cadon stopped in his tracks and turned to face her. "I have to go, Mal. It's my sister. My mom's already lost my dad. I can't let her do this on her own."

"But... what if something happens to you?"

The rest of the team had moved on ahead of them now and were almost to the office building. A thousand ideas of what could happen to him on the inside of the tunnels filled his mind. Cadon realized that this might be the last time he ever looked into those beautiful violet eyes. "I'll be careful," he assured her.

Tears filled her eyes. "We're just getting to know one another. I don't think I can do this without you."

"I know. I'll be back." His heart hurt in his chest as he saw the raw emotion in her eyes. Just like in Alcatraz, Mallory was scared. Not just for herself and her future–but for him.

Acting on instinct, Cadon tipped his head down and brushed his mouth over hers. Full and warm, her lips felt perfect against his. She pushed up onto her tiptoes, pressing against him, and the urge to kiss her more deeply fought to the surface.

But he didn't. He could hear Elliott shouting at him to come on and knew he had to go. "I'll be back," Cadon whispered. He brushed a few tears off her cheek.

"I'll be waiting for you," she assured him.

With a smile, Cadon ran a hand through her silky dark hair and turned to head to the office building, more determined than ever to get into those fucking tunnels, find his sister, and get home.

16

Jo

THE WOMAN with the bright red hair looked up just as Jo realized who she was. In her arms, she cradled a baby, and a huge monster was about to snatch them both up into its dinosaur-like maul.

Jo raised her gun to shoot the damn thing, but before she could, shots rang out from the other direction, the area closer to where the monsters seemed to be coming into 'the beyond,' and the giant creature hit the ground, causing a reverberation to shake the ground under Jo's feet.

She still rushed in that direction, wanting to help Aislyn and Aarolyn in any way she could, and maybe get a closer look at her baby sister.

Before she reached them, her father hurried over. "You've got to get home," he said, helping his wife up. God, here that woman was his wife.

"I know," she said in a thick Irish accent. "I'm trying to. Thank you." She leaned over and kissed Jo's father, and her heart fell into her stomach.

"I need to get this portal closed, and then I'll be there. Be careful!" Aaron looked up, probably checking to see if there was anyone around who could escort his wife and daughter home, but then his eyes met Jo's, and his expression changed. "What the fuck?"

"Hi, Dad." She swallowed back her anguish from before. The idea that he was happy here, that he had no reason to want to go through the tunnels with her, faded from the back of her mind where it had started to take up residence.

"Jo? Did you come through–"

"No," she cut him off. "I mean… yes. But not on purpose. Something grabbed me and pulled me through."

"Oh, god." Aaron shook his head. "Are you okay?"

"I'm fine for now, but I need to get through that portal into the Blood Moon tunnels before you close it. And so does…." She turned around to see Ryker with his arms around a woman and two little girls, and once again, her heart lurched, though this time, she had no reason for such a response. "Ryker."

Aaron looked over and saw him. "Are you sure he wants to go?"

"He says he does."

"Who–who are you?" Aislyn asked, her forehead crinkled.

Aaron bit down on his bottom lip, shifting his weight from side to side. "This is… Jo. My other daughter."

"Hi." She managed a forced smile as she nodded at the woman who had married her dad first–sometime around the Irish Potato Famine. She was the woman he'd had to kill because she'd become a vampire. Her gaze settled on her sister's face. Aarolyn smiled and reached for her, completely oblivious to the danger going on around her. Instinctively, Jo reached over and wrapped her hand around her chubby fist. "Hello there." She'd never been interested in babies before, but this one was different. This girl should've been her big sister. Instead, she'd be a baby here in 'the beyond'–forever. Questions of how it was determined how old everyone was when they got here slipped her mind as her father began to speak.

"Aislyn, I'm going to have to take Jo home."

The petite redhead's eyes bulged. "But… we need you here."

"You'll be okay without me until I can get back."

Confusion washed over Jo as she tried to determine what her dad was saying. Was he talking about getting her through the tunnels to the other side and then coming back the same way he went out? But that would be so dangerous. Or… did he mean something else? If they exited 'the beyond' through the Blood Moon Portal tunnels, there'd be no danger of Demonic Vampires being unleashed into the world.

He could go out with her. He could go home—to her mom.

Aislyn let out a sigh. "Will we remember you?" Tears filled her eyes.

"I don't know," Aaron admitted. "I don't know how long I'll be gone either. But I have to make sure she gets home safely. I'm sure you understand." He wrapped his hand around the back of Aarolyn's head, and she cooed up at him.

"I'll give you a moment." Jo took one more look at her baby sister and then stepped away. While she waited for her father to finish his conversation, she surveyed the area. More monsters continued to pour through the portal opening, but several LIGHTS team members stood near the glistening hole that seemed to be formed in midair now, and most of the creatures weren't making it to the city proper.

In the distance, Jo saw a woman with long dark hair and wondered if that might be Brandy. She hadn't turned around yet, but something told Jo that was her.

She also saw a man in a Revolutionary War uniform using what appeared to be a modified musket to mow down the monsters. When he turned to look over his shoulder, she saw his face and recognized him from that corpse in the tunnels. Alexander Hamilton.

"Jordan?" Aaron called behind her, and Jo's great-grandparents both rushed over. She couldn't hear what her father told them, but she imagined he was asking them to escort his family home. He also gestured over to where Ryker was kissing Claire, and Janette nodded. A moment later, Ryker let her go, hugged his little girls, and rushed over toward her, wiping a tear from his eyes.

Ordinarily, Jo would razz him for crying, but under the circumstances, that wouldn't be appropriate at all.

When Ryker reached her, Jo asked, "Are you sure?"

"Stop fucking asking me that," he growled. Then he turned to Aaron. "Nice to see you."

The Guardian Leader's forehead puckered. "Are you a... Guardian?"

"Crazy what a little Transformation serum in a Blood Moon Portal can do." Ryker smiled, but Aaron wasn't amused.

"I didn't see you outside of the portal opening. How did you get in here?"

Before Ryker could come up with an explanation, Jo chimed in, "He's rescuing me." She shook her head, still annoyed that Ryker had followed her through. "We need to get to mom before she does something stupid and tries to come after me." With that, she took off toward the portal opening, knowing her father and Ryker would follow.

The closer they got to the tunnels, the more monsters they encountered. The three of them worked together to take down several, including a wolf-lizard creature and a flying lobster that almost took Ryker's head off.

"Brandy, Alex! We need your help," Aaron shouted to the two closest LIGHTS members. At least, Jo assumed Brandy had once been a member.

"What's goin' on?" Brandy asked in an accent that reminded Jo a bit of Heather's.

"We've got to get through the portal, and then I'm going to close it," he explained.

"You're going through?" The alarm in Alex's voice was evident. "But... how will you get back?"

"I don't know, Alex, but I've got to get my daughter home." Aaron shot a charging hippo with the face of a cat.

Jo met Alex's eyes, and he blinked a few times before replying, "Understood."

"It'll be impossible for you guys to fight yer way through that tunnel," Brandy said, shooting another monster.

"We'll figure it out." The confidence on her father's face left little room for argument.

Still, Brandy questioned, "How the hell did this happen anyway?"

"Fucking Christian Henry," Jo blurted, shooting another monster.

"What?" Brandy's voice raised a couple of octaves.

Jo turned to look at her and noted the woman's eyes were wide in shock. Clearly, this was the same Brandy that Christian had a picture of on his desk. Jo had no idea what their relationship had been before the woman died, but by the irritated look on her dad's face, she guessed he did.

Either that or Aaron was just reacting to knowing that all of this misery had been brought on by the same pain in his ass who'd been plaguing him for decades.

Why couldn't Christian just die?

"You remember him, Brandy?" Aaron asked, recovering from his exasperation.

The brunette nodded. "Yes—now that I've heard his name. Why would he do such a thing?"

"I have no fucking idea," Jo admitted. She turned to look at her father. "But it had to be him. When I told him that Mom was planning to talk to you, he disappeared into the tunnels."

"I wouldn't put it past him." Aaron killed another monster, and they all moved closer to the portal opening.

"I'm coming with you." Brandy's voice sounded determined as she killed a snake-like creature slithering toward her boot.

"No, Brandy." Aaron's tone was authoritative as he shook his head. "It's too dangerous."

"Besides, if I have my way, he'll be here soon enough," Jo added. From what she'd gathered, everyone ended up here, regardless of whether or not they were assholes. Somehow, Vampires were here, like Aislyn, but it was as if they'd never been turned into the evil bloodsuckers. That must be what went to hell. The urge to look around for some delightful version of Holland almost had her head turning, but she didn't. Ryker kept putting himself into compromising positions, and she was afraid he wasn't going to even make it into the tunnels with them.

"You want to kill him?" Brandy's face paled even further.

"Yes." It wasn't difficult for Jo to admit it. "After this, absolutely."

"Let's worry about getting that hole plugged up and getting you through hell and back to your mom," Aaron suggested. "Then we can worry about Christian."

"But he's in there," Jo reminded him. "He probably did this just to stir things up. Asshole."

"I don't know why he did it," Aaron admitted, shooting his way closer to the portal opening. All of them were forced to shoot monsters as they got closer to the hole. "Until we know what's going on, there's no reason to plan anyone's demise. Brandy, I don't think it's a good idea for you to come, but if you are, then let's go."

A smile formed on the brunette's beautiful face. Jo shook her head. Why would anyone give up paradise for fucking Christian Henry? Unless, of course, Brandy also wanted to kill him.

"Ryker, you go through first," Aaron ordered. "Clear the path for the women, and I'll come in after you."

Before Ryker could respond, Jo said, "Dad, I'm fully capable of–"

She didn't get to finish. "Damnit, Jo, just do as you're told for once," Aaron barked at her.

Taken aback, Jo said nothing else and prepared herself to fight her way back into the tunnels–or hell–whichever it was waiting for them on the other side of the portal opening.

Ryker peered through the hole, raising his weapon and shooting a few rounds in. Jo wasn't sure if he saw anything or was just trying to keep the onslaught of monsters at bay. Satisfied that the situation was as good as it was going to get, he stepped through the gleaming circle and quickly disappeared.

Jo swore a few times under her breath and then followed him, her gun at the ready.

The moment she moved inside, she began firing at a large bat-like creature that had launched itself at Ryker. He was lying on the ground in front of her, struggling to break free of the talons sunk deep into his shoulders. Jo shot the monster several times, and it finally fell to the ground.

Before Ryker could even get up, another monster was headed at them. She stepped out of the way of the opening and fired several times and then heard gunfire coming from behind her. Both her dad and Brandy were through the portal now.

"Where are we?" Brandy asked, shooting another monster.

"This is the Blood Moon Portal." Jo recognized the black tunnels. "But it's so fucking hot in here, we have to be close to hell."

"Let me get the portal closed, and then we'll figure it out," Aaron said. "Cover me."

The three of them moved into position behind and around him. Jo had her back to her dad, so she couldn't see what he was doing. She had to hope the watch he was wearing would still work the way it had before he died and wore it to 'the beyond.'

For some reason, the monsters weren't coming as quickly now as they had been before. Whether they sensed their way out was now closed or whatever had been sending them this way had stopped, she couldn't say, but Jo only had to shoot one large creature before she heard her father's voice again.

"Done."

She spun around to see the hole to 'the beyond' was closed. Taking a deep breath, Jo wiped her brow on the back of her hand and surveyed the scene in front of them. Would it be possible for her father to just open a portal now for them all to get out, or was Christian already out of the tunnels? If that was the case, one of them would be left behind.

She couldn't let that happen. She needed to find Christian.

17

Cadon

By the time Cadon reached Christian's office, everyone else was already there. Along with Emma and Lucy, they were talking over one another, trying to figure out who was going to do what.

HIs mother's voice was both the loudest and the most frantic. "I really don't give a fuck about getting trapped in there again," she said. "I just need to get in there and find my daughter!"

"There's no way in hell we're going in there without a fucking Vampire," Elliott retorted. "We have to make sure everyone can get out."

"We don't have time to find one right now!" Cadence countered.

Cadon found himself in a position he'd never been in before. While he completely understood both sides of the argument, he knew someone had to take charge of this situation and come up with a plan, and the people who generally did that were all arguing at the moment.

"All right–listen!" he shouted. "This is what we're going to do." Remarkably, everyone else quieted and turned to look at him. Most of them stared back at him with bulging eyes, as if they didn't know he was capable of speaking up.

Cadon took a deep breath as his aunt smirked at him. "Okay—Mom, Elliott, Jamie, Zane, Cassidy, and Brandon, you're going in to find Jo and Ryker. Lucy, Ashley, Scott, and I will go find a Vampire—somewhere outside of campus. Someone who hasn't turned to us for help. Emma and Hannah will stay here in case Christian comes out. Once we have the Vampire, we will go in, make sure the Vampire can't escape, and then find you."

"How are you going to get in without the watch?" his mother asked, her voice calmer than it has been since Jo disappeared.

"Emma will keep the watch here. I know that means you won't be able to get out before we come in, but then, you couldn't all get out anyway if Christian leaps somewhere. He could come out anywhere in the world." Cadon thought of those coordinates his sister had found in the desk. That had to have been part of Christian's plans at some point. He'd definitely thought about where portals were easily opened.

"It'll be hard to find you in there," Zane said. He was one of the more recent people to have visited the portal.

"We can use our IACs," Elliott pointed out.

"Let's plan to meet in the center hub," Cassidy added. "That'll be the easiest place to find."

Cadon didn't know what he was talking about, but he felt like it would make sense once he was inside.

"Are you planning on asking Scott to come with you inside?" Jamie asked. "He's not going to like that, and I'm not sure I want my whole family in there."

"He has to have a Healer with him," Cadence weighed in before Cadon could even answer.

"I was thinking Ashley could help us find the Vampire, but she should stay here. I'll convince Scott to go with me." Cadon felt confident in that. "Besides, he's the only one who's been in there."

"Dax," Brandon said quietly. "He said he'd never go back, but he might if it means finding Jo."

Cadon nodded. "I'll send him a message. Now, you guys should get in there and find Jo before she gets hurt."

"Weapons!" Elliott murmured. He ran out of the room, and Jamie followed him. A few moments later, he came back with a buttload of guns and ammunition. Ashley and Jamie followed, their arms wrapped around one another.

"Be careful!" Ashley told all of them. She kissed her husband, and then looked at Cadence, an unspoken message passing between them.

"All right. Let's go." Cadence took a Beretta from Elliott and slung it over her back before nodding at Emma.

With a nod, Emma lifted up the watch, and a moment later, the air in front of them began to shimmer. Cadence stepped over and kissed Cadon's cheek. "Be careful."

He promised, "I will."

Then, his mother stepped back through the hole into the place where she'd been imprisoned for a decade. The others on her team followed suit, Jamie the last to leave as he lingered with his arm around his wife.

When they were all gone, Emma clicked a button or two on the watch again, and the portal closed.

Ashley began to sob, and Lucy moved to her, wrapping her arms around her. "It'll be okay," she promised.

"I know. I just hate that any of this happened." Ashley wiped her eyes and shook her head. "Okay. Jamie said we're on Vampire duty?"

"That's right," Cadon told her. "Let's get Scott, and then we'll go out and find a bloodsucker we can take into the tunnels with us. Hannah and Emma will stay here on portal-duty in case Christian comes out."

Ashley nodded and sniffled a bit. "I'll send Scott a mind-link message to meet us outside. We are going to need some chains. I saw some in Jamie's office we can grab on the way out."

The question of why Jamie would have chains in his office sparked in his brain, but then, who the hell knew what kind of messes the Healer had found himself in. Elliott had left a few of the guns they'd gathered on Christian's desk. Cadon picked one of them up, weighing it in his hand. "Then, let's go."

Lucy was already armed, as was Ashley. While he was confident that this first job would be easy, as they bid goodbye to the other two women and headed outside, Cadon was leery of what he was going to have to do next. He'd hoped he'd be able to avoid going into those fucking tunnels, but it seemed like his luck was about to run out.

Ashley ducked into Jamie's office, and then they headed toward the doors. Stepping outside into the night air, Cadon took a deep breath and tried to clear his mind. He'd somehow presented himself as a leader to this group, even though he had the least experience and didn't really want to lead anything. He looked to Ashley, the oldest and most experienced of the three of them, hoping she'd take the lead.

Instead, she asked, "Where to, boss?"

"I have no fucking idea," he admitted. "We need a Vampire who hasn't recently tried to come to us for help, someone who still wants to cause trouble. I wouldn't feel right leaving anyone in there who wanted a reprieve."

"There might be some down on Prospect Avenue," Lucy offered. "That place was infested with them before we overthrew the government, and it's always been a place to find trouble."

"All right." Another deep breath didn't do anything to calm him. "Let me message Dax. We need a… car."

Ashley raised an eyebrow. "Cadon, are you all right?"

"You seem a little lost, bro," Lucy added.

"I'm fine." it was an instinctual answer, not a true one. He ran a hand through his hair. "Just… thinking."

"I'll go get an SUV and pick you guys up here," Ashley offered. She reached over and patted Cadon on the shoulder. "I'll message Scott while I'm gone. Maybe we should take him with us. Just in case."

Cadon's head nodded even though he hadn't processed everything Ashley had said just yet. Too much had happened in too short of an amount of time for his brain to work through all of it. His sister was gone. His mom was back in the tunnels. His dad was still dead. And he'd kissed Mallory.

Shaking his head in an attempt to clear it, Cadon used his IAC to reach out to Dax. *"Hey, we have a huge problem we need your help with."*

A moment later, the Guardian replied, *"What's that?"*

"Jo got sucked into the Blue Moon Portal. We think Christian opened a portal into 'the beyond' to let the monsters from hell through, and one of them grabbed her. Mom and a bunch of other guys went through a portal to try to find her, but we need to take a Vampire in with us." It was all a jumbled mess he probably wasn't going to understand.

It took Dax a full minute to reply. *"What are you saying, Cadon?"*

Swallowing hard, Cadon put all the cards on the table. *"I need you to go into the Blood Moon Portal with me to find them."*

"Fuck no." This time, his answer was quick and decisive. *"Absolutely no fucking way am I ever going in there again."*

"Dax, it's different this time. We'll have my dad's watch. We can use it to open a portal to get out anytime."

"No. I told everyone I would never go in there again. You can't fucking make me."

Inhaling sharply, Cadon ignored Lucy as she asked for an update. Headlights in the distance told him that Ashley was almost back, and he saw Scott heading their direction from the apartment building.

Maybe he didn't need Dax. After all, Scott had been in the tunnels before, and both Ashley and Lucy were capable and didn't seem afraid. Still, he'd been instructed to bring Dax along, and with everyone else in his family gone, he was kind of in charge here. Was he going to put up or shut up?

Gritting his teeth, Cadon replied, *"It wasn't a request, Dax. We are going to find a Vampire to take into the tunnels with us to leave behind so we can all get out. I'll be back in an hour or so. Meet me in Christian's office. If you're not there, there will be consequences."*

Fully expecting Dax to clap back with some sort of a response that reminded him Cadon hadn't even been born the last time Dax was in the tunnels, he disconnected the IAC call before the Guardian could do so and marched off toward the SUV. Ashley pulled along the curb as Lucy trailed him.

"Cadon? What is going on?" she repeated.

"Nothing. I just told Dax to meet us back here in an hour." He did his best to sound nonchalant, but fear and irritation gripped him, tightening his gut into a knot.

"Does he not want to go?" she asked as Cadon slid into the back seat, leaving shotgun for Scott. Lucy climbed in beside him.

"It doesn't matter," Cadon replied. "For better or worse, I'm in charge here now, so he'd better be there when we return."

"Damn." Ashley laughed and waited for her son to close his door before peeling away, headed for the exit to the compound. "That's the sort of McReynolds gumption we're used to."

Cadon wanted to tell them not to get used to it, but he bit his tongue.

"I know we're going to get a Vampire to meet Dad in the tunnels, but that's all I know," Scott said, not bothering to hook his seat belt even though his mother was driving at least seventy. "What the hell is going on?"

As they made their way across the remains of Kansas City toward what had always been one of the rougher parts of town, the three of them filled Scott in on what was happening. He, too, seemed a little tentative about going into the tunnels again, but he knew that his father was in there, so he didn't balk on saying he'd go, especially since he knew his mother would absolutely be going in.

The closer they got to the area of the city they were headed toward, the more the buildings around them showed signs of distress. Many of them hadn't been in good shape before the Revelation, but with the Vampires taking over, there was no one to take care of them. Roofs sagged. Paint peeled. Plants reclaimed the territory that had previously been theirs before civilization moved in. Street lights flickered or didn't work at all. This was the sort of place that would make most people turn around and drive away as fast as they could.

Cadon wasn't afraid of Vampires, especially not with Scott nearby. He'd be able to fix anything that might go wrong pretty quickly–for the most part. And Cadon had enough experience fighting the bloodsuckers now that they were the least of his worries. Going into the tunnels and fighting creatures he'd never seen before, as well as potential demons from hell, that was scary.

Ashley pulled into a parking lot, and the four of them got out, quiet and still as they looked around, feeling for that familiar tingle that would announce a Vampire was nearby.

It only took a few seconds before Cadon recognized it. At least one Vampire was lurking in the shadows of the abandoned pub to their left. There could be several. He hoped so because they weren't trying to destroy this bastard–they needed this one alive.

"Come on," he said, moving in that direction. With the other three on his heels, Cadon led the way. It was an unfamiliar and unwelcome place for him to be, but as a McReynolds, it was nearly impossible for him to find a place in the back. For better or worse, like it or not, he was in charge.

He just needed to find a way not to fuck it up.

18

Jo

"It's hotter than hell in here," Ryker quipped as the four of them began to make their way toward the glowing red light in front of them. Since the portal had been closed, no more monsters had approached them. The impulse to rush this area of the tunnels must've faded with their opportunity at freedom.

Jo checked her IAC, hoping she'd spot Christian somewhere within the complex of tunnels, but the only other LIGHTS team member who had a little glowing light in her eye was Ryker, which wasn't much help since he was right beside her. Frustration set in. She knew they were going to have to walk through at least a portion of hell to get out of there, and she wasn't excited about it. She'd just been here a couple of weeks ago, and it hadn't been pretty. She did remember that the creatures tended to leave them alone when the natural openings of the portal occurred. Otherwise, they'd be all over them shortly.

"Can we just pop out and pop back in again somewhere else?" Ryker asked.

"I would like to get you and Jo out of here as quickly as possible," Aaron admitted. "But I have a feeling she's not going to budge on leaving me in here. Without knowing whether or not Christian is still in here, we won't know if we can all get out until we try. Believe me, it's not a pleasant experience when you hit that wall that keeps you locked inside."

Jo swore under her breath. "The quicker we find Christian, the better. Asshole."

Brandy made a low meeping sound behind her, and Jo wondered if she found her characterization of the major offensive, but she didn't care. They wouldn't be in this mess if it wasn't for his selfishness.

She wanted to ask Brandy how she knew Christian, but she decided now wasn't a good time. They were getting closer to the red glow, and that meant trouble.

"Dad, have you ever been in the hell portion of the tunnels before?" she whispered.

"Many times," Aaron replied, not keeping his voice down, like he knew something she didn't. "It's mostly the same creatures as elsewhere, but they're pissier. We shouldn't have to go past the place where the Vampires hang out. But then, with Christian in here wreaking havoc, who the fuck knows what we might run into."

In the distance, Jo heard a hissing sound which almost seemed like a Demonic Vampire letting the Guardian Leader know what awaited them.

"I don't understand," Brandy mumbled. Jo turned and looked at her quickly before returning her attention to the glowing portion of the tunnel ahead of them. The feel of the black rock beneath her boots was unwelcome in the way sand at the beach wedging its way between her toes had always been a sensory nightmare. Once they got past hell, into the other portion of the tunnels, she'd be more comfortable opening a portal and getting out. Then, maybe she could find some LIGHTS team members to help her capture a Vampire and throw it inside so whoever stayed behind from their party could get out. She selfishly hoped it was Brandy who got left behind since she didn't even know the woman. But anyone who would leave heaven to be with Christian Henry had to have some mental issues.

She knew it wouldn't be this stranger, though. A good leader would never let one of his team members stay in the tunnels while he went home–and her father wasn't just a good leader.

He was the greatest to ever live–or die.

Since no one else responded to Brandy's utterance, Jo took it upon herself to do so. "What do you not understand?"

"How Christian could do something so… vile," she replied. "I know he's not the nicest person ever born, but why in the world–"

"He's an asshole," Jo said, not for the first time. "I've never met anyone outside of a Vampire who is as vindictive and hateful." She turned to look at the other woman and saw her eyebrows raised in shock. "I guess he wasn't always like that?"

"Has been as long as I've known him," Aaron added.

The cowgirl took a deep breath and blew it out slowly. "I guess things changed after… after I died."

"How did you die?" Ryker asked from Jo's left. She didn't bother to turn and look at him since she needed to keep an eye out on the shifting shapes in front of her.

"It was all a set-up." Brandy's tone filled with remorse. "I thought I was saving my own ass with what I did to Christian, but in reality, I was just getting rid of him for our boss's sake–and then that bastard took me out, too."

Confusion washed over Jo as she stopped walking and turned to face the other woman. "Wait a minute. Are you saying…?"

Brandy nodded. "That's right. Christian's probably pretty pissed at me right now. Since I'm the one that killed him."

Jo stared at her, wide-eyed, for several seconds, trying to process and think of a response, but then she heard a screeching noise behind her and realized she wasn't going to be able to ask any questions about how this woman had killed Christian. As she spun to fight whatever was coming at them, she mumbled, "Lucky bitch."

Ryker shot another black creature, and it fell hard enough to shake a few pebbles loose from the ceiling above them. This one looked a bit more human, but it was large and furry—still the color of the sky between the stars at midnight.

"Shall we?" Ryker asked, his tone full of sarcasm as usual.

The party continued, the orange glow becoming brighter as they made their way toward whatever ring of hell they'd have to go through to get to the door that led to the tunnels with the hub, the area she was more familiar with. Her father wasn't intimidated at all to proceed, and Jo trusted him.

A thousand questions flooded her head as she walked. How many times had he come through here when he was looking for her mom? Had he walked right over that portion of the tunnel that opened up into the floor beneath and not known it? Was there anyone else down there?

The answer to that one she was fairly certain was a no. If Christian got out through a portal opening before they got through to the area where Aaron was more comfortable opening a portal, one of them would be stuck.

Her eyes darted to Ryker. He had that stoic look on his face, his eyes crinkled, his shoulder-length blond hair messy from all they'd been through, tiny beads of sweet clinging to his forehead.

Why had he come through the Blue Moon Portal to save her? Perhaps more importantly, why hadn't Zane? He'd been right there with her, holding her hand, his arm around her, as they spoke to her dad through the blue, misty haze.

Where had Ryker been?

None of it made sense to her.

Her thoughts were interrupted as they rounded a corner, and the glow intensified. A cavernous area widened in front of them, and up ahead, to her right, a large pool of orange liquid bubbled up from the ground creating a pool of intense heat in the shade of molten lava.

"What the fuck?" Ryker muttered. "I never saw anything like this before."

"It's a deterrent," Aaron explained. "While it is possible to get around it, most of the creatures that occupy that area over there won't come through." His blue eyes surveyed the area in the distance before he turned toward the narrow path to their left and in front of them that skirted the pit of fire.

"Are the monsters we've been fighting coming from down there?" Jo pointed in the same direction Aaron was now walking.

"Most likely. They're tunnel monsters, nothing too terrible." The Guardian Leader led the way, and the path was too narrow for them to even double up. As Jo went behind him, more concerned about something–or someone–jumping out from in front of them and mowing him down than anything else, she stayed close to the wall on her left. On the other side, the ground sloped down gradually to the bubbling orange pool. Steam rolled off the edges, smoke rising and burning her lungs with a sulfuric odor. Beyond the pool, more tunnels led in more directions than she cared to count, and all of them glowed a bright red.

No, she hadn't made it this far into hell the last time she'd been in the tunnels, and she'd prefer not to ever come this way again.

The path ahead led out of the orange chamber and into one more the color of the sky at sunset. The path widened up, and Jo stepped up to walk beside her father, her gun at the ready. While there was another pool of fire here, it wasn't as large or bright. Neither was the cavern itself, and the tunnels on the other side weren't as red either.

"Seems like a more reasonable area of hell," Ryker muttered right behind her.

An awkward giggle escaped her lips. "Maybe more your speed?"

"I think I belong a bit deeper." His voice was a raspy whisper that gave Jo pause. Had he meant that to sound so… sexual? Probably not. Not with her father standing right next to her. Out of the corner of her eye, she saw Aaron's right eyebrow twitch and knew he'd not only heard it but was equally surprised at Ryker's innuendo.

Choosing to accept he simply meant he was a bad boy and nothing more, Jo took a few hurried steps to usher them on their way. They hadn't seen any monsters for a while, but they had to be around here somewhere. She constantly trained her eyes along the overhangs and jutting rocks around them, looking for beasts and Christian. Or maybe there was no delineation after all.

"Wish we had some water," Brandy mused behind them. "This place reminds me of the desert. Any of you been out there when the sun is blazing down on you? Damn, it's hot."

Jo knew exactly what she was talking about. She'd been out there hunting Vampires a time or two, but she couldn't do much more than nod. She could go for a cold glass of water about now, too.

"Shit," Aaron mumbled, picking up speed. She knew he could outrun all of them and probably would've made it to the central hub if he didn't have to stick with the rest of them, but she didn't know what he was irritated about until a tell-tale whooshing noise hit her ears.

Had he heard it before her or sensed it?

It didn't matter. That must be the indication that the portal just closed its natural opening, and that could only mean one thing.

They were about to have company.

19

Cadon

THE STENCH of urine and pot filled Cadon's lungs as he entered a building that appeared to have been a bar at one time. All that was left, other than a dilapidated chunk of wood with shelves behind it and a few random tables and chairs, was a neon sign on the wall with enough broken glass it would've been impossible to read even if it had been plugged in.

Their boots crunched on broken beer bottles, pipes, and probably needles. Cadon chose not to look down, but when Scott murmured, "You've got to be shitting me—literally," and began to wipe the bottom of his boot off on the windowsill, Cadon spared a few hazardous gazes down at the path in front of him.

The intense sensation that there were multiple Vampires nearby intensified as they moved through the building. Most of this refuse was left over from human inhabitants, but they were long gone—or long dead. No, the stirring inside of him was a clear indication that there were Vampires here.

But where the fuck were they hiding?

121

Two doors were visible on the right side of a narrow hallway toward the back of the establishment with a third on the other side of the hallway. He assumed those were the restrooms and some sort of a storage closet. Behind the remains of the bar itself, another door probably led to some prep area for staff.

Cadon continued across the floor, waiting for someone to tell him what to do, when he remembered he was someone.

"Ashley, take that door behind the bar," he instructed, since she was the one closest to the entryway. *"Lucy, the door in the hallway on the left. Scott, I've got door number two."*

"Copy," Scott said as the women also sent their confirmations through the IAC.

With a deep breath, Cadon rushed toward the door he'd assigned to himself and waited for Scott and Lucy to fall into place. *"Go."* Maybe that wasn't the signal his dad would've given, but it worked, and all four of them punched through the barriers in front of them, guns drawn, ready to shoot.

It was then that he remembered shooting wasn't the objective. *"Numbers?"*

Before anyone spoke, gunfire rang out all around him as his colleagues obviously took in similar scenes to the one he saw before him–four male Vampires pouring out of a stall, fangs bared, claws at the ready.

"Fuck!"

Despite his knowledge that they needed to take one of these bastards alive and everyone was shooting, Cadon did the same, firing at all of them as quickly as he could pull the trigger. With Holland dead, it wasn't nearly as difficult to kill the assholes as it used to be. Smoke and ash puffed into the air as he blew the head off one pale older fellow with dark eyes and inch-long fangs. Next, he shot a thinner vampire with blood stains on his shirt in the chest. He, too, puffed away.

The third stocky fellow took two bullets to the gut before Cadon hit him in the heart, ending him, and he hit the fourth, taller with a mop of unruly red hair, in the shoulder before his brain began to function properly again.

The Vampire took a few steps backward, running into a urinal, a thin trail of smoke curling around his alabaster face as he shrieked, grabbing his wounded arm.

It was clear none of these bastards were experienced fighters, and all of them were weak. Otherwise, it would've been more of a fight. His teammates began shouting numbers in his head, but Cadon stayed focused. He didn't need to know how many Vampires they were killing if he took this one in alive himself.

Grabbing him by the front of his shirt, Cadon rammed the bloodsucker's head into the mirror. It shattered instantly, flecks of glass tinkling to the ground as the Vampire shouted again. Raising a clawed hand, he grabbed hold of Cadon's fist, sinking his talons into his flesh, but Cadon didn't let go. He spun the Vampire around, ramming him into the urinal again before he took him to the ground. The scent of raw sewage mingled with the ash, and bile bubbled up in the back of his throat, but he swallowed it down and crushed his knee into the Vampire's tailbone.

"Just fucking end me!" the monster shouted.

"You're not that lucky, asshole." Cadon yanked his left hand behind him, continuing to keep his full weight on his body, and then reached for his right hand, the one that had been digging into his own flesh a few moments ago. It took some work, but he managed to unwedge it from the ground and yank it around behind him, too.

"Where the fuck are those chains. Ashley?" Cadon shouted through the IAC as the Vampire who had just been begging to die a few moments ago attempted to find a way to claw his way out from under the Hunter.

"Did you get one?" Ashley slammed through the door, the sound of rattling chains accompanying her. "I accidentally fucking killed all of mine."

Cadon didn't answer because he couldn't. He was about to lose his grip on the asshole's arms. Blood from his own wounded hand slid down between his fingers, coating them in a sticky mess that somehow also made them slippery.

Ashley dropped to the ground beside him and began to wind the chains around the Vampire's wrists. "These are the ones Christian made," she explained. "I can't remember what he used to make them, but he shouldn't be able to break free. Especially without that extra surge of power Holland used to give them."

"Let me die!" the Vampire begged as Cadon resituated his grip further up his arms so that when he stood, he was hauling him up, too. "I want to fucking die!"

"You think you wanna die now," Ashley replied. "You just wait."

Cadon held him in place as Ashley wound the remainder of the chains around the Vampire's middle, securing his hands so that he couldn't easily break away. As she did so, the monster elongated his teeth and opened his jaw far wider than any human ever could, attempting to bite her face. Cadon clubbed him in the head, and the Vampire whimpered, his head swinging to the side.

"Need some duct tape or something?" Scott asked from behind him.

"Do we have any?" Cadon took hold of that disheveled mop of hair and pulled back tight enough that the Vampire was looking up at the ceiling.

"I'll find something!" Lucy shouted, her boots crushing more glass as she rushed back to the supply closet.

A few moments later, she returned with duct tape. Ashley had finished her job, so she helped Cadon hold the bloodsucker's mouth clamped at an uncomfortable angle as Lucy and Scott wound the tape around his lower face and up around his head. They used most of the roll in an attempt to make sure the bastard didn't break free.

Once they were finished, Cadon loosened his grip slightly and let out a deep breath. "That was easier than I thought it would be."

Ashley snickered as if she thought he was being sarcastic, but he actually meant it. "Glad someone managed to grab one and not just shoot them all."

"Same," Lucy agreed. "Hey, your hand is bleeding pretty badly."

Cadon looked down and saw several puncture wounds that started at his knuckles and ended near the wrist of his left hand. It hadn't hurt that much until he looked at it. Now, the throbbing pain intensified with every passing second. He wasn't used to getting hurt in the field. He usually stood far enough back that he was never anywhere close enough for a Vampire to get him.

"I'll fix it." Scott placed his hand next to the wounds, and a gentle blue light radiated out from his palm. It took almost a full minute, but the wounds closed, leaving no trace that they'd ever been there at all.

With a nod, Cadon said, "Thanks, Scott," and placed his hand back on the chains behind the Vampire's back, moving him toward the door. While he was grateful that the pain had stopped, this was just a reminder that Scott's healing powers were not as powerful as his father's—not by a long shot. Cadon thought of how Scott hadn't been able to save his dad and wondered what the hell was going on inside of the tunnels.

The Vampire struggled to get away from them as they transported him back through the bar and out onto the sidewalk. The sensation that eyes followed him as he made his way to the SUV had Cadon looking around, but if there were more Vampires around, they were safe from LIGHTS for now. He didn't have time to go hunt down any other bastards tonight.

As tempting as it was to throw the Vampire in the back by himself, Cadon knew they couldn't risk taking their eyes off him until he was in the Blood Moon Portal in a position where he wouldn't be able to get out or die until they got all of the LIGHTS team members out—except for maybe Christian. He placed the Vampire in the middle of the back seat and instructed Scott to sit on the other side.

With the women in the front, they headed back to headquarters. A glance at the clock in his IAC told him they'd actually be there before the time he'd told Dax to meet him.

They'd just pulled up in front of the office building when Cadon heard a frantic voice through the IAC. *"What the fuck are you jackasses doing over there?"* Margie Joplin demanded, her name flickering to life in the corner of his eye.

Confused, Cadon asked, *"What are you talking about?"* The rest of his team got out of the SUV. He'd have to find a way to direct the Vampire into the building while answering Margie's questions, something he'd never been too good at.

"Did someone go through the Blue Moon Portal?" she wanted to know. *"One of my elimination squads just intercepted what appeared to be a Demonic Vampire coming into a small town on the outskirts of Melbourne. That's the same fucking place where Carter and Holland came through."*

Cadon swallowed hard. His first impulse had been to ask her why she was contacting him, but it would be impossible for her to get in touch with Jo right now, and everyone had been told to leave Cadence alone unless she reached out to him.

By default, he was the McReynolds in charge. *"Yeah, but it wasn't on purpose,"* he began. *"Christian Henry busted a hole into 'the beyond' while we were talking to Dad, and a bunch of monsters poured out of the Blood Moon Portal into heaven—or whatever it is. One of them grabbed my sister."*

"The actual fuck!" Margie exclaimed. *"That's insane! That bastard deserves to die. Why would he do that?"*

"I really don't know his reasoning." The Vampire refused to walk, and Cadon found himself kicking the asshole in the back of the legs as they stumbled toward Christian's office. *"Did you catch the Vampire?"*

"Catch her? Fuck no," Margie answered quickly. *"I told them to rip her fucking head off."*

Cadon took a deep breath and let it out slowly. *"That works, too."* They'd all been warned that Demonic Vampires were incredibly hard to kill, so he was surprised that it hadn't been that difficult, or at least, it didn't sound like it had been. He only had a vague idea of what an elimination squad was, but he assumed Margie had formed teams to go out into the towns and kill every Vampire they encountered. Since Australia's government had never toppled to the bloodsuckers the way the United States had, they were better equipped and organized to do so.

"That's it, then? Just Jo? No one else came out or went in? Jeez. How the hell are you going to get her out?" Margie's tone softened slightly once her rage at what she'd probably assumed was incompetence ended.

It was about to flare up again. *"You might have one more,"* he admitted timidly. *"Ryker went through to help Jo. We're trying to get them out through the Blood Moon Portal, but I don't know if it's going to work."*

The string of expletives pouring through the IAC was enough to make him blush despite being a grown ass man. *"I'll let my people know,"* she finally said before ending the call.

Cadon didn't even care that he hadn't gotten a chance to tell her to keep him updated. They were in Christian's office now where an extremely disgruntled Dax glowered at him, and Emma had the watch ready to open the portal. She gave him a quick lesson on how to use it–how to make sure they got back to the office when it was time to come home. He nodded, hoping he would remember under pressure.

"All ready?" she asked, smiling at him like he was about to embark on an adventure on a magical school bus.

"As I'll ever be."

2 0

Jo

RUNNING at a full sprint in an attempt to keep up with her father, Jo managed to stay ahead of Brandy by quite a distance, and it was clear Ryker was doing his best to keep behind the brunette who'd clearly never had the benefit of a second Transformation shot–if she'd ever had one to begin with. She might've Transformed naturally. Her speed, or lack thereof, made her a liability, and Jo could tell her dad was annoyed because he kept glancing over his shoulder at them.

"Why the fuck are we running?" Brandy asked between panting inhales.

"That sound means the portal just opened." Ryker could talk and run at the same time since he was really only jogging at this point, she assumed without turning to look at him. "We need to get away from hell."

"Why?" Brandy clearly didn't understand, but when the path ahead of them widened a bit, and the orange glow gave way to more of the black ash, Aaron slowed down.

They still hadn't crossed through the door that led them out of

129

hell, but Jo recognized this place. She'd followed Cassidy this far. She slowed down, too, and glanced around her. It would likely only be a matter of moments before–

An eruption of gunfire in front of her had her spinning around to see what her dad was shooting at. Sure enough, an onslaught of creatures came rushing through the path that led back to the tunnels. A menagerie of twisted, dark monsters so thick they could barely fit down the path came barreling toward them. All four of them opened fire, Aaron dropping down out of the others' way, likely in an attempt not to get shot again. Jo moved to her right and Ryker followed while Brandy ducked left. Though they were taking out a lot of the larger creatures, the smaller ones were obscured by the crowd, making them harder to shoot.

Jo watched as Aaron dodged around what she swore looked like a dog with a clown's head, and then she lost track of him as a whale cow swam right at her, almost knocking her down.

Ryker emptied his Glock into it, which meant he needed to reload. As soon as she regained her balance, Jo stepped between him and the onslaught, shooting as fast as she could. Eventually, the mele tampered down, leaving her squatting with one leg extended, trying to catch her breath.

"Are you okay?"

Ryker's question made her realize she'd zoned out a bit. Popping up, Jo shook her head. She had no idea where her dad or Brandy were, and neither of them had an IAC. "I'm fine. You?"

"Yeah, no thanks to you," he muttered, checking his weapon but not putting it away.

"What the fuck is that supposed to mean?" She spun to look at him, the same bitter taste of annoyance that always filled her mouth when they argued, coating her tongue.

"How do you miss a fucking whale cow?" Ryker started to walk further down the tunnel the way they had been going when the mayhem had broken out.

"I didn't miss it," Jo argued, rushing to stay caught up with him. The tunnel narrowed here, making the dim light from the orange lava pits far behind them less useful. Shadows separated her from Ryker, and all she could see was the slight gleam of his blond hair.

"You didn't kill it," he mumbled.

"Hey!" She sped up and grabbed his shoulder, turning him to face her. "You make absolutely no fucking sense, you know that? All we ever do is bicker at one another. Most of the time I think I fucking hate you, and then you jump through a goddamn portal for what? To save my ass? Why didn't you just fucking stay there?" Movement behind him caught her attention, and her finger itched to pull her weapon, but then she realized it was her dad. He was about twenty yards ahead of them.

"Brandy took off," Aaron shouted. "I'm going to look for her closer to the door. I'll meet you there. Be careful."

"You, too," Jo called as Ryker dragged a hand down his face and spun away from her. "An interruption is not a reprieve," she reminded him.

A rumbling laugh deep in his throat was all she got in response.

Irritation had her balling her free hand into a fist, and all she could picture was slamming it right into the back of his stupid fucking head. How dare he prance around like she owed him something because he'd been idiotic enough to follow her through the portal?

"Hey!" Jo shouted again, grabbing his shoulder. This time, he swiped her hand away. "Ryker, you owe me an answer!"

"I don't owe you anything, Josephine," he replied. "Let's just get out of here alive so you can get back to your boyfriend."

The way he spoke of Zane, it seemed clear he wasn't fond of the guy, yet she had no idea why. Zane was always nice to everyone, probably the nicest guy, the nicest human being, on the planet. So why did she find herself saying, "He's not my boyfriend."

"Your fuck-buddy then." It was a growl akin to the sound the monsters made when attacking.

She couldn't argue with that, could she? They did have sex most nights. But it wasn't like that's all they were doing.

Was he her boyfriend?

Confusion washed over her until she realized this was all a distraction. A howl in the distance reminded her that they weren't out of trouble just because they were away from the lava pits. She still couldn't see her father, had no idea where Brandy was, and there was no indication on her IAC that anyone else was in here with them, which was weird.

Where the fuck was her mom?

The anger she'd felt before when he'd stormed away from her hadn't died down, though. It wasn't like Jo not to get answers when she wanted them. "So you're just going to walk away from me like a little fucking baby, is that it?" she taunted. He'd take the bait and turn to talk to her. She knew he would.

Ryker stopped in his tracks and slowly pivoted to face her. "Yeah, that's what I'm doing right now."

"Why?"

"Why what? Why am I walking away from you? Because I'm trying to get you out of here, and since it seems like the cavalry ain't coming, it's up to me."

"You don't think I can take care of myself?" She folded her arms and stepped back against the wall.

"If the whale cow incident is any indication, or the octopus that sucked you into the portal to begin with, I'm going to go with no. Besides, the guy who has the watch that can open the portal just went that way, so—"

"My dad won't leave me in here." She resented the implication that he would ever do such a thing.

"I don't think he would either, but if he gets killed—again—or something eats the arm he uses to tell time, well, we're in trouble, so let's just go."

Ryker turned to walk away again, but she reached out to grab him. "No! I'm not taking another step forward until you tell me what the fucking deal is!"

"What the fucking deal is?" he repeated.

"Yes!"

"The fucking deal is—" He swiped his hand through his hair

roughly enough to pull some of it out. "Goddamnit, Jo, I'm falling in love with you–and I don't want to."

"You're what?" Her eyes widened in shock at his revelation. What was it about these goddamn tunnels that made everyone think they loved her? She was still trying to come up with some sort of a response when time slowed to a crawl as she watched Ryker's eyes bulge and his entire body stiffen. His hands shot out to his sides, and he started to levitate up and away from her.

Confused, Jo only stared for a moment until she saw what looked like a sword sticking through his chest, right in the center near his breastbone. Gasping, she tried to ascertain what was happening as the point opened up into a thousand fingers.

Something had him from the back–and she needed to kill it before it killed him.

Ryker reanimated at the same time that Jo realized what was happening. He reached for the appendage that had speared him as she darted behind him to find a squid-like creature with wings attempting to stab him again.

Jo opened fire at such close range it only took a few shots for the monster to stop moving. A piece of shrapnel hit the tunnel wall and ricocheted off, hitting her in the face. The sting and feel of blood dripping down her cheek didn't deter her as she quickly moved to pull Ryker away from the corpse. As she pulled him free of the spear, a sickening sucking noise made her stomach roil. Ryker's mouth fell open as he gasped in pain.

"Sorry! Sorry!" She had no idea what else to say, but it had to be done. The tentacle fell to the ground with a wet thunk, and Ryker was free.

But he was bleeding like a sieve. The front of his white T-shirt was already coated in blood, and she imagined the back was just as bad. If they didn't get him help right away, he was going to die.

Jo looped his arm around her shoulders and started walking toward the door to hell as fast as she could. She needed to find her dad and get the portal open so they could get to a Healer before he bled to death. Otherwise, Ryker was a dead man.

She heard the sound of her dad approaching at the same time tiny flickers of light came to life in her mind's eye. So many names and IACs flared to life at the same moment, she didn't have time to register them all. But one stood out, and she would've smiled if she didn't think she was about to burst into tears.

"What the hell happened?" Aaron asked as he took Ryker's other arm.

"Monster," was all she could say as they rushed Ryker forward. It would be safer to open the portal on the other side of the door–but maybe they didn't have to yet.

"*Mom!*" Jo shouted through the IAC. *"Please tell me you have Jamie with you!"*

21

Cadon

WALKING through the portal was nothing like what Cadon expected. For some reason, he'd imagined it would be a pretty instantaneous transport. One moment, he'd be standing in Christian's office, and a step or two later, he'd be in the infamous tunnels he'd heard so much about.

But that was not the case. As he dragged the Vampire behind him, he followed behind Lucy and Ashley, with Scott and Dax behind him, for what seemed like a mile before the waving lights around them finally gave way, and they stepped through to the darkness of the Blood Moon tunnels.

The ashy ground crackled beneath his boots as he followed the women forward. Neither of them had been in here before either, but it seemed like it was pretty straightforward. The tunnel headed in one direction only, at least at this entry point. He checked his IAC and felt a wave of relief to see his mom was still in here—and so was his sister.

"I have no idea which direction we are going," Scott admitted. "But

I think if we keep following the tunnel, we'll hit the hub. Either that, or we're going the wrong way, and we'll hit the outer loop."

"What happens if we hit the outer loop?" Lucy asked, her weapon pointed out in front of her and her finger on the trigger, like she would mow down anything that moved.

"Be careful," Cadon interrupted. "We've got teammates in here."

"I'm checking IACs," Lucy confirmed. "If Christian Henry pops out, I'm shooting his fucking head off."

"Noted." Cadon gave the Vampire another commanding tug as he tried to dig his heels in. They'd readjusted the chains and taped a bag around his head in the office before they'd come through, but he was still being uncooperative. He wished they could just dump him and walk away, but he understood the importance of keeping the bastard alive until they all got out.

"If we hit the outer loop," Scott continued, as if he hadn't been interrupted, "we'll just turn around and go back the other way. Most of the tunnels aren't that long, but some of them wind around."

"And how will we know if we're about to be attacked?" Ashley asked.

"We won't." Dax's tone conveyed his anger at having been forced back in here. "You usually feel the bite before you see the teeth."

"That hasn't been my experience," Scott replied, "though I suppose that's possible."

Dax didn't respond, only growled. Not for the first time, Cadon questioned whether or not he should've brought him along. If he wasn't going to be helpful—like leading the way or carrying the Vampire—he should've stayed back at the office.

"*Mom, where are you guys?*" he asked through the IAC.

"*Oh, good. You're here,*" she replied. "*Well, we are currently rushing to the door to hell. Apparently, Ryker's hurt, and he needs Jamie.*"

"Shit." Cadon wasn't sure what else to say. The barrage of questions he wanted to ask died down with that information. "*Should we meet you somewhere?*"

"*Just head to the hub, but don't step out into it,*" she told him. "*Do you have the Vampire?*"

"Yes." As if he sensed his fate was being discussed, the bloodsucker bucked again. Frustrated, Cadon jabbed him in the back with his elbow.

"You know, we could just cut his fucking arms and legs off. That would make him easier to carry," Lucy suggested.

"I'm thinking about it," Cadon admitted. That made him a bit more cooperative, but it was still abundantly clear that the Vampire didn't like this trip any more than the rest of them. Probably less.

"We'll need to take him to the level where Holland had me imprisoned to make sure he doesn't get out before we do," Cadence explained. *"I'm not sure how to get there. Jo knows."*

"Okay." It was clear she was distracted, so he decided not to say anything else to her. "Mom said we have to find some secret layer of tunnels to dump this asshole, but she's in a rush to go help Ryker."

"Ryker's here?" Ashley glanced over her shoulder, her eyebrows arched. "I figured he just went through so that he could be back with his family."

"I have no idea," Cadon admitted.

"Why would he go through all the trouble to become a Guardian if he wanted to be with his dead family?" Lucy questioned.

"Don't ask me. Maybe he didn't want to die, but then, when he had the opportunity, he took it." Ashley shrugged. "Why else would he go through the portal?"

"To save Jo," Dax answered, making all of them pause for a beat before they continued on their way. "Come on. I don't hang out with either one of them, but I can tell he's got it bad for her."

The idea of anyone having the hots for his sister made Cadon's stomach tangle, even though he obviously knew she spent just about every night screwing Zane. Still, this was something different. Zane was Jo's... boyfriend? Wasn't he? Ryker was... not. "What makes you say that?" His tone was more aggressive than it needed to be, and he thought he heard Lucy snicker in response.

"They fight all the time," Dax pointed out. "They've been at each other's throats since the moment they met back in Russia. Come on. It's pretty obvious to anyone with a brain."

"Guess I left my brain in my other pants," Cadon mumbled, getting another giggle out of Lucy who clearly loved anything sarcastic.

Before they could further discuss whether or not Ryker wanted to do his twin sister, a haunting howl echoed off the tunnel walls all around them, sending a chill down Cadon's back. He'd never heard anything like that before. It sounded like the ridiculous noises amusement parks used to simulate what they supposed a ghost might sound like.

"What the fu–" Lucy didn't get the rest of the word out before she opened fire. In front of them, several large creatures rushed down the tunnel. In the dim light, it was difficult to make out their exact forms, but none of it made sense to Cadon's mind anyway. Parts and pieces of various animals seemed to have been soldered together to make new creatures–all of them with large teeth and claws and the overwhelming need to rip apart anything that got in their way.

Cadon raised his weapon to shoot, but he couldn't get a clear target on any of them, and the Vampire began to buck and try to pull away from him at the same time, either sensing the onslaught or in an attempt to use the precarious position as a means to escape.

"Keep that asshole safe, and we'll cover you," Scott told him as he turned to shoot similar creatures that were coming from behind them.

With very little choice, Cadon dropped to the ground with the Vampire, using his full body weight to keep the bastard from wiggling away from them. "Do you want me to feed you to a snake with hands?" he snarled, knowing the Vampire couldn't answer. The sharp rock floor cut into his hands and knees as he struggled with the asshole. The option of cutting off all his limbs grew more acceptable by the moment.

After what seemed like forever, but was probably only a few minutes, all the creatures were either dead or limping back to wherever they hung out when they weren't trying to kill people.

"That was… interesting." Ashley didn't holster her weapon, but she did relax a little. "Everyone all right?"

"I got nicked, but I'm fine," Lucy told them, shaking her arm. Scott stepped over and placed his hand on what appeared to be a scratch mark on her arm that was deep enough to rip through her leather jacket. In a moment, she was fine and thanked the Healer for his assistance.

"Hopefully, that's the worst wound I have to heal while we're in here," Scott said as he reached a hand out to help Cadon up.

Looking at Dax, Cadon said, "Stop him if he tries to limp away."

Dax nodded, but it was clear the attack hadn't made him any more excited to be here.

As Cadon got up, the Vampire attempted to scoot away. Dax reached down and grabbed him by the chains, yanking him up pretty easily. Cadon thanked him and went back to the routine of hauling the asshole around.

"Where are we going again?" Lucy asked.

"To the hub," Cadon told her as they stepped over the carcasses of the monsters. It seemed they were starting to disappear into the black rock of the floor. Scott grabbed the Vampire's other side to lift him over the larger creatures.

"Have you been to the hub before, honey?" Ashley asked her son.

"Yep," Scott replied. "See that opening up there?"

Now that Scott had mentioned it, Cadon could see where they were headed. He wished he would've thought ahead to bring a flashlight, but then, that might've just been a beacon to the monsters to tell them where they were located.

"What do we do when we get there?" Ashley asked.

"Try not to get killed until someone can show us where to take this bastard," Cadon explained. "Mom said not to step into the hub."

"Is it dangerous?" Lucy slowed down as they neared the end of the tunnel.

"It can be," Scott told her. "The monsters down any of the tunnels can see you if you're in the hub. And then there's the fact that a lunatic is potentially prowling through these tunnels trying to kill all of us."

Cadon nodded. His friend was right about that. He wouldn't put it past Christian to kill any one of them–except for his mom. He didn't think Christian would kill her.

But then, he really had no idea what the hell the bastard was capable of.

They'd just come to a stop near the exit of the tunnel and taken a pause to catch their breath when Cadon caught movement out of the corner of his eye. He had to turn his head and look at the creature coming out of the tunnel across the way because he'd never seen or heard of anything like it. Clutching onto Scott's arm, he asked, "What the actual fuck is that?"

Scott gasped and whispered back, "I have no fucking idea."

"Those," Dax began, his breathing so labored he sounded like he might pass out at any moment. "are demon hunters. Run!"

22

Jo

"HE'S BLEEDING BADLY, MOM!" Jo practically shouted through the IAC. They'd made it almost to the door to hell before they'd had to sit Ryker down. He was losing too much blood to continue, and her dad had agreed they needed to stop and put pressure on the wounds.

"*We're almost there,*" Cadence said back in her head.

Jo balled up Ryker's shirt in the front and pressed it against the gaping wound, pushing hard enough that she hoped it would help in the back, too. "They'll be here soon," she whispered.

Ryker nodded. "I have an IAC, too."

She narrowed her eyes at him but didn't clap back. She had her visuals on now and saw her mom and Jamie sprinting ahead of everyone else as they headed for the tunnels. In a few seconds, her mom would be there, and she'd see her dad again for the first time in over a decade.

Ryker's face was so white, it practically glowed in the dark tunnel. She had no doubt he'd be dead soon. Tears clouded her eyes as she fought to think of something to say to him, but nothing came to

141

mind. All she could think about was what he'd told her right before they'd been attacked.

He'd said he was falling in love with her.

Was she falling in love with him, too?

She was so close to him now, it would be easy to lean in and tell him that she didn't know for sure, but she wanted him to stick around long enough to find out. With a deep breath, she whispered, "Listen, Ryker, you can't die, okay?"

He blinked a few times like maybe he had heard her, or maybe he hadn't. "It's just as well," he muttered. "You're with Zane."

"I know. We are close, but he's not my boyfriend. I honestly don't know how I feel–"

Before she could finish her sentence, a blood curdling scream sounded somewhere in the distance, possibly back the way they'd come. Immediately, Jo reached for her weapon, but her dad said, "That was Brandy," letting her know it wasn't an imminent attack. "I thought she was ahead of us." He looked toward the door to hell before turning and peering behind them. "I'll be back."

"Dad, no!" Jo shouted after him, but he had already taken off, a streak of black leather against the darkness of the tunnel walls. "But Mom is almost here!"

Of course, he didn't stop. If he thought he could help someone else, he'd put his own needs off to do so. Swearing under her breath, Jo returned her attention to the IAC in time to see her mom and Jamie busting through the door to hell. She could hear their footsteps now as they neared, and then Jamie's blue light radiated over both of them. She scooted out of the way so that the Healer could rush to take her place. A moment later, her mom's arms were around her. She buried her head in Cadence's comforting shoulder and let tears fall for the first time since her dad had died. "It's okay, honey," Cadence said, rubbing her back. "Jamie will fix him."

"I know," Jo muttered. "But…." She lifted her head to look at her mom, but behind her, she saw someone else. Someone who looked like he had just had his heart ripped from his chest.

Zane.

Confusion washed over her as Jo tried to ascertain why he would look so upset. After all, he'd never been a huge fan of Ryker's, though they'd managed to get along. But then she realized exactly what had happened.

The fucking IAC.

Her eyes widened, and she pulled away from her mom, taking a few steps in the Guardian's direction, but he backed away.

"I'm going to go help Cadon," Cass said from somewhere to Jo's left. She couldn't pull her eyes away from Zane's to comprehend who else was standing in the tunnel. "He's run into some demon hunters, and he doesn't know where to take the Vampire."

"I'll go with you." Zane's tone was icy and almost completely void of emotion–except for a hint of bitterness.

"Wait, Zane!" Jo took a few more steps toward him, but he just shook his head and stormed off, falling into step with a few other people Jo didn't register as Cassidy led the way back toward the door to hell.

"I should go with them," Cadence said. "They won't know where to take him. I'll need to find that opening–"

"No!" Jo practically shouted in her mother's face as she started to turn away, and she realized her mom hadn't been paying close enough attention to what was happening as she was barreling toward them to register that she hadn't been alone with Ryker.

"What is it? You're with Jamie. You'll be fine." Cadence reached up and brushed the tears from her cheek.

Shaking her head, Jo said, "Dad."

"Wh-what?" Cadence took a step backward and hit the wall of the tunnel. Absently, she reached up and brushed the back of her head, like it hurt, but she didn't feel it. "Wh-what about him?"

"Cadence?"

Jo stepped back out of the way as her mother's head turned in slow motion toward the sound of her father's voice. The sound she made was a cross between a whimper and a gasp as her hands shot up to cover her mouth. She pulled them away as she moved toward his open arms, but not another sound came out of her mouth before his lips met hers in a kiss that would've made Jo blush even if they weren't her parents.

Snickering, Elliott said, "It's like the Cliffs of Moher all over again." Jo had no idea what he was talking about, but it didn't matter. Her parents were together once more. She took a deep breath and thanked whoever might be watching over them.

"You came back," Cadence whispered. Jo could only hear her because her IAC was still on.

"I did."

"Promise me you'll never die again." She leaned up to kiss him again before Aaron could answer.

When she finally let him go, Aaron said, "I'll do my best."

"Hey, can the rest of us get in there or what?" Elliott stepped over to hug her dad, and then Jamie did the same.

Looking down, Jo saw Ryker trying to pull himself up to standing. "Hey, careful there!" She leaned down to help him. "You were mostly dead a few moments ago."

"I'm fine," he assured her, all the grumpiness swiftly returning to his disposition. "Did you find Brandy?"

With the question, the happy reunion stopped. Aaron shook his head. "No, I have no idea where she went. It's like she just fucking disappeared."

"Asshole opened another portal," Elliott surmised. "He probably took her and hopped back into the real world."

"Dammit," Jo whispered. He was likely right. Christian had probably gone back into the offices, taking Brandy with him. With any luck, Hannah would head them off, and he'd be dead by the time they got back home.

"We have two watches now," Elliott pointed out. "Why don't the four of you go home and let us handle making sure the Vampire gets placed and everyone gets out okay?" He was clearly talking to everyone but Jamie, who was too powerful of a Healer to leave everyone else behind.

The four he'd been referring to all answered in unison. "No!"

Elliott's eyes widened, and he backed up a step. "Why not? You think we can't handle this?"

"Our son is still in here," Cadence reminded them. "Jo, you and Ryker should–"

"No." She looked into her mother's eyes. "My brother is still in here, and so is… Zane." She wasn't even sure she should be allowed to say his name after what he'd overheard. Ryker cleared his throat, and she wondered if he realized what they'd done or if he'd been too out of it. The shitty feeling she'd been overwhelmed with up until her parents' reunion was back with a vengeance.

"All right, well, let's go find everyone else. We need to stick together and keep each other safe." Aaron immediately hopped right back into Leader mode, which Jo appreciated. She'd just as soon never take that role again if she could help it.

"I just hope we're not leaving Brandy in here," Jo mumbled as they headed toward the door to hell.

"I'm sure Christian must've gotten her out of here," Elliott said. "Why would he stick around–"

Before he could finish his thought, their IACs all flickered a few times and then went off.

Everyone stopped in their tracks except for Aaron who bumped into Jo's back and then stopped because he still had his arm around her mother who was no longer walking. "What's going on?" he asked.

"Our IACs. They died. All at the same time." Jo looked at Elliott, Jamie, and Ryker, who weren't behind her, and they all nodded in agreement. "What would cause–"

"Fuck!" Aaron groaned. "He's not gone. He's still in here somewhere. Bastard."

"What do you mean?" Jo turned to look at her dad. He dragged his free hand down his face. It was enough for her to ascertain that he was talking about Christian, but she didn't have enough information to put the pieces of the puzzle together.

"IACs didn't work in here the first time we were trapped," Jamie explained. "I wasn't really expecting it to work now, but I guess

Christian rigged something?" He looked past her to Aaron who nodded.

"That's right. I thought he'd planted it somewhere in the hub, but knowing him, he moved it." Aaron shook his head again. "He's fucking with us."

"There's got to be a reason for that," Elliott ascertained. Looking at Aaron, he said, "You need to go home, man. You're the one he wants dead."

"I wouldn't put it past him to kill any and all of you," the Guardian Leader retorted. He looked at his wife, "Except for maybe you, and then I'm not so sure."

"Can we find it and turn it back on? Cadon's gonna need it to find us." An uneasy feeling settled in the pit of Jo's stomach. This was bad. It was like they were in a funhouse, one full of ghosts and goblins, and an overlord was fucking with them.

"We'd probably be better off finding everyone else and getting out of here," Aaron said with a deep breath. "But that means that Brandy is probably still in here somewhere. I thought that scream came from behind us, but these tunnels echo, and it's possible she already went through the door during that last attack. We need to get to her soon."

"If she's still alive," Elliott mumbled. "She killed him the first time, right?"

Aaron nodded. "Yes. I thought he loved her, and she didn't have much of a choice, but he's such a sadistic bastard, who the hell knows what he might do?"

"Let's head to the hub and reassess. We just need to be careful. There's just one of him, and there are six of us," Ryker said, all of his strength apparently restored.

"One of him and seven thousand demons," Jamie reminded them. "And apparently those fucked up demon hunters are back."

"I didn't see much of them in all the years I spent in here," Aaron told them as they started cautiously proceeding toward the door again. "They look like something out of a horror novel, but I don't think they're dangerous."

"I hope you're right since the last thing I heard from our son before the IAC went dead was that they were being chased by a group of them," Cadence replied.

Jo took a deep breath and followed behind Jamie and Elliott, next to Ryker, with her parents behind her, hoping they all managed to get out of there safely. She'd already spent a bit of time in 'the beyond,' and that was enough for her–for now anyway. Maybe one day she'd want to go back, but not today.

Not anytime soon.

23

Cadon

"WHAT THE FUCK just happened to our IACs?" Cadon rushed down the tunnel with the rest of his party in front of them, hauling the Vampire on his back, those fucking demon hunters closing in on them quickly. Their gossamer-like bodies floated through the air, their eyes glowing in the darkness as they seemed to shift shapes like mist over a lake at dawn. Only their furry white feet, which drifted over the ground more than stepped, seemed tactile.

Not that any of them wanted to reach out and touch one. Dax told them he'd encountered the bastards the first time he'd been in the tunnels, and they were not to be trifled with. Whether or not they'd ever hurt a Hunter or Guardian, he couldn't say, but Cadon hoped none of them would be the first to find out.

No one answered his question, and he didn't expect them to. Their IACs had flickered and then turned off as they reached the end of the tunnel. A small outer loop wrapped around the outside of the tunnels on this end, with the hub taking up the middle. A few of the tunnels had adjoining passageways, but for the most part, walking through them was like being lost in a massive cave that never seemed to end.

Until he needed this one to continue and it didn't.

Rather than joining up to the other tunnels, this one ended with a massive cave-in of black rock that had them trapped.

"What the hell happened here?" Ashley asked, panting from the run.

"This must be where Aaron and Christian set those grenades off to kill the demons when they were trying to get out that first time," Dax explained.

The whooshing noise of the three demon hunters that were coming from the other direction had them all spinning around, weapons drawn.

"Should we try to shoot them?" Cadon asked.

"You tell us. You're the boss!" Lucy had her weapon out in front of her, but she hadn't fired yet.

Indecision paralysis took over before Cadon finally managed to say, "Shoot them! Shoot them!" as the closest one bore down on them.

All five of the LIGHTS team members opened fire on the wispy creatures. The one in front roared but didn't stop coming, and the bullets seemed to pass right through them.

When the creature's arm hit his face, Cadon sputtered and moved to the left, closer to the wall. Wet and spongy, the demon hunter felt a lot less threatening than it looked. When it made contact with him, it made a low rumbling noise in the back of its throat, like it was trying to ascertain whether or not he was friend or foe.

Cadon didn't want to stand around and find out whether or not it meant to attack. Giving it a shove in the opposite direction, he hugged the cave wall and pushed past it, shouting at the others, "Let's go!" The Vampire on his back slammed into the wall hard enough to make him meep in pain, but Cadon didn't slow.

Seeing their bullets do nothing inspired the rest of the team to go with this strategy as well. Sputtering and gasping, the five of them shoved the unusual beings out of their way and managed to get past them back down the tunnel a ways before they heard a whooshing sound that had Dax screaming a litany of curse words.

"What was that?" Cadon stopped in his tracks, but the howling and grunting they'd heard earlier picked up in intensity.

"That was the portal opening," Dax whispered.

Slowly, Cadon turned his head to see the demon hunters flying back at them. Their countenances had changed from inquisitive to angry. "Get down!" he shouted. Dropping the Vampire to the ground, he climbed on top of him in an effort to protect their precious commodity. The rest of the team hugged the floor as the three misty creatures went screaming past them, the high-pitched noise reverberating off the black walls.

Lying on his stomach with the sharp rock biting into his knees, Cadon took inventory of himself and determined he was okay, other than a few cuts and scrapes. Should he pause to assess his life's choices at this point, he might've felt less unscathed.

"Everyone okay?" Ashley asked, getting up.

"Fine," Lucy said, dusting her pants off as she stood next to Ashley and Scott who'd popped up next to his mother.

Cadon rolled over and pulled himself up, leaving the Vampire on the ground for now. "Yeah." He didn't care to elaborate, and when he saw Dax wasn't moving, alarm filled him. "You okay, man?"

"No!" Dax didn't lift his head. His face was buried in his hands, and Cadon could see blood coming from his arm, though it didn't seem like much. He checked with Scott who only shrugged in confusion.

"What's the matter, Dax?" Lucy crouched next to him while Cadon and Ashley turned to keep an eye out on the tunnel in front of them. He tried to remember which direction they'd come from when they'd taken off running from the demon hunters, but then, didn't the tunnels shift positions whenever the portal opened?

"I want to go home!" Dax moaned. "You guys don't understand. The last time I was in here, I had no idea when I was going to get out, and Tara...." At the mention of his dead wife's name, Dax burst into tears. His shoulders heaved as he tried to suck in what little air could flow between his hands and his face with his head scrunched so close to the lava rock-like floor. "She didn't know where I was."

Cadon looked at Ashley and Scott, and both of them nodded. They needed to let him go home.

"There you are!"

The sound of his aunt's voice pulled Cadon's attention away from the sobbing Guardian. He couldn't remember a time when he'd been happier to see her. Brandon and Zane trailed behind the Hybrid as she flew down the tunnel and came to a stop in front of them. "Demon hunters didn't get you?"

"No, but I think the tunnel floor bit a chunk out of Dax," he replied, hoping to explain what was going on with the man on the ground.

Cassidy's forehead crinkled, and she slowly shook her head. Something told Cadon she had more insight into what was actually going on here than Dax had told them. "Do you have Aaron's watch?"

"I do." Cadon lifted his wrist to show her.

"Great." Taking a deep breath, she bent down. "Dax, why don't we open a portal and send you back to the office? You can have Cale look at those cuts, all right?"

Slowly, Dax lifted his face. Blood streaked his cheek, but it was from his hand, nothing serious. "I'm sorry, Cass. I just... miss her so much."

"I know." Cassidy took a deep breath, and Cadon thought he saw a tear forming in her eye. "I do, too. I think you've been enough of an asset on this journey, and it's time for you to head back." She straightened up and looked at the rest of the team. "Any volunteers to make sure Dax gets back safely?"

Cadon didn't expect anyone else to abandon the mission, so he was shocked when Zane said, "I'll go with him." He stepped past the rest of the team to squeeze his tall frame between Cadon and Cassidy.

It was then that it registered how odd it was that he was with Cassidy and Brandon anyway. He knew he'd heard his sister's voice over the IAC right before the demon hunters had entered the picture.

Had something happened that he'd missed? Shouldn't he be smooching Jo and praising the heavens that she was back?

"Thanks." Cassidy definitely knew more than he did. "Cadon, do you know how to open the portal?" She helped Dax up off the ground as Cadon fumbled with the watch.

"Mom, you should go back, too," Scott pressed. "We're good now."

Ashley shook her head. "I don't want to leave you in here, especially with the IACs not working. I'm not sure where your dad is."

"He's right inside the door to hell," Cassidy explained. "Ryker got hurt. He's fine now, I think. The rest of the team is together. Brandon and I can take this fucker down to the other layer and keep him there until everyone else can get out. Shouldn't take long now."

She seemed confident in her assessment, but Ashley's mouth was moving with no noise coming out, an indication she wasn't sure what she should do.

"I can fix the IACs, I think," Lucy chimed in. "I remember seeing some information about how Christian got them to work in here on his computer. If the device he set up is still in the hub, I should be able to get it restarted, assuming he didn't completely trash it."

"See, Mom? Everything's fine." Scott patted her on the back. "I'll be home before dinner."

"It's the middle of the night—"

"Before breakfast." Scott nearly rolled his eyes at the mom-like expression Ashley was giving him. "I think Dad and I would both feel better if you were back in the office helping Hannah. Besides, there's a good chance Christian bailed on us and is already back there wreaking havoc."

Ashley tilted her head to the side, and it was clear she didn't think Christian was at the office. But when Dax started crying again, her motherly instinct kicked in, despite the fact that she was about the same age as Dax, as far as Cadon knew. "All right. Let's go." She looped her arm through Dax's and nodded at Cadon.

With a deep breath, he looked down at the watch. It was difficult to see the details in the dark tunnel, and he was afraid he'd fuck it up, but then Scott lifted his hand, and a soft blue light illuminated his wrist enough for him to see the right buttons. Emma had left it dialed to the correct coordinates, and when he clicked the buttons on the side… nothing happened.

"What the fuck?" he muttered, looking at it more closely.

"I think it's both of those two." Lucy pointed at the two buttons he'd just pushed.

"That's what I did," Cadon assured her.

"You have to… just try it again. At the same time."

"I did it at the same time." Cadon pushed the same buttons again, a little harder this time, and the end of the tunnel began to dance with the lights that indicated the portal was open.

"Good thing you got some practice in. Just in case the next time is an emergency." Brandon clapped Cadon on the shoulder as Dax and Ashley stepped through, disappearing from sight.

Zane took a step forward, but Cadon grabbed his shoulder. They'd never been friends, but the guy had been in his living space quite a bit lately. Something was off. "You okay?"

Zane turned to look at him, a deadness behind his eyes the likes of which Cadon had never seen. He gasped and took a step back. Zane only nodded, and then he was gone.

After a few seconds, the portal closed on their end. Cadon had no idea how much time they had to get through or how any of that worked, but Cassidy didn't seem alarmed, so he didn't either.

Not about that, anyway.

"Poor guy." She shook her head.

"Dax?" Cadon asked.

"No, Zane. Did you not hear what your sister and Ryker were talking about? They blasted it to the whole team." She folded her arms and took a deep breath.

"No, I was too busy running for my life," Cadon admitted. "And I guess we don't have time to get into it now. What's the plan?"

"Why the hell are you asking me? You're in charge here." His aunt had a taunting look in her eyes.

Cadon sighed. "Fine. You and Brandon are taking this fucker off my hands since you can float his lazy ass. You know where you're going?"

"Yeah. Cadence came up in tunnel thirteen. We'll find it, pop down there, and drop him off."

That worked for Cadon. "All right. Lucy and Scott will go fix the machine that makes our IACs work because otherwise we won't be able to coordinate getting out of here."

"What about you?" Lucy asked.

Taking a deep breath, Cadon replied, "I'm going to stand guard while they're down in the other layer, just in case Christian shows up and tries to fuck things up."

"Couldn't he just use his watch to make a portal down there?" Lucy asked.

"I honestly don't know, but I feel like things are about to get turned on their ear again, and this is my best guess as to how I can be useful," he admitted.

"Let's do it." Cassidy patted him on the shoulder and then used her powers to pick the whimpering Vampire up off the ground, and the teams moved out.

Cadon hoped his gut was wrong, but he didn't feel that lucky.

24

Jo

A FEW MOMENTS after they walked through the door to hell, they were near enough to the hub that Jo could see the tunnel widening out in front of them. Something was off, and she didn't want to just step out into the middle of such a wide area with no plan.

Everyone seemed to feel the same way. At the edge of the opening, Jamie and Elliott stopped and turned to face them. "Christian might be waiting in any of the tunnels to ambush us."

Aaron stepped past Jo, and once again, she was glad her dad was there to take charge. "We need to split up. I know there's a device somewhere in here that we can use to turn the IACs back on, but I have no idea where it's at. We can break into teams, send a group to try to find it, but we also need to locate everyone else. Including Brandy."

"Cass was going to find Cadon. I'm sure she'll take care of the Vampire," Cadence offered. "Jo, do you remember which tunnel you found me in?"

"Yeah, it was thirteen," she said confidently. "So she's probably headed that direction. Do we think the rest of the team will go with her or come to the hub?"

"I think Lucy will try to turn the IACs back on," Jamie offered. "She knows more about that sort of thing than the rest of us."

"Honestly?" Jo took a deep breath and leaned back against the wall for a moment. "I think Christian is going to try to find you, Dad. I don't think he's going to walk out of here without you dead. Again."

Aaron's blue gaze met her eyes, and for a moment, Jo remembered what it was like watching him die the first time. She could not do that again.

"You should go." Cadence's voice was just a whisper. "Please."

He shook his head. "I can't do that. I can't leave you guys in here and hide. Besides, if he wants to kill me, he'll keep coming until he finds a way."

"But he can't kill you in the real world," Elliott argued. "Not after you've already died once."

"We don't know that," the Guardian Leader pointed out. "We know you can't die again because you went through the Blue Moon Portal. But I didn't."

"I don't want to find out." Jo folded her arms and looked down. She felt the nudge of Ryker's arm against her but couldn't look at him.

"As long as we are all together, he won't be able to take us all out," Jamie said. "So let's try to stay together."

Everyone agreed with that, and with weapons drawn, they stepped toward the hub—just as the tell-tale whooshing sound hit their ears. A litany of curse words also filled the air as the screeching and howling began.

Within a few moments, a barrage of demons was bearing down on them from every direction. The team had no choice but to fan out so that everyone could take aim without the risk of hitting one another. Jo found herself in the opening of a tunnel with Ryker and Elliott, the three of them shooting as quickly as they could. It seemed like there were more creatures to kill this time, and they didn't stop coming.

Across the expanse of the hub, she saw Jamie sticking to her father like glue, which gave her a bit of comfort as she took out a devil-dog-looking monster. Some kind of possessed rabbit leaped at Cadence, who hadn't strayed too far from her husband, its teeth clamping down on her arm. She ended it with the twist of a blade, and Jamie blanketed her with blue light almost immediately.

A few moments later, the creatures slunk away. Jo took a deep breath and leaned against the wall, trying to calm her racing heart. Somewhere in one of the distant tunnels, she heard a smattering of gunfire and assumed that was another part of their team. The creatures didn't always attack just when the portal was opening; sometimes they struck without warning. It was possible the fight was left over from the opening, or perhaps another group had run into a stray monster. Either way, she hoped her teammates were all right. If something happened to Zane before she had a chance to talk to him….

"You all right, Jo?" Ryker asked, reloading his weapon.

"I'm fine. Is everyone okay?" she called to her parents and Jamie.

But it was Elliott who answered. "Never fucking better. We should really locate tunnel thirteen and get the hell out of here before–"

His sentence was interrupted by another bloodcurdling scream. This one didn't echo off the walls quite as much and sounded closer by. "Help! Please, someone! Oh, God!" a woman's voice shouted.

Jo locked eyes with Elliott, then Ryker, before they all turned their attention to Jamie. He had to go–didn't he?

"Fuck," the Healer mumbled. "Where do we think she is?"

"Sounded like it came from that way to me." Elliott pointed across from them and a little to the left.

"Elliott, go with him," Aaron ordered.

"But don't you think–" the Guardian began to protest.

"I'll be fine," Aaron interrupted.

"I'll go." Ryker was already moving in Jamie's direction without so much as a glance at Jo, which was just as well. Everything was awkward now anyway.

Since Aaron didn't insist it be Elliott, the two Guardians headed off together, rushing down the tunnel they surmised the screaming may have come from, and then Jo and Elliott moved back to where her parents were standing.

"What now?" Elliott asked. "Thirteen?"

"Thirteen," Cadence nodded. She stepped over to the closest tunnel with Elliott right behind her. "What the fuck is this anyway?" She pointed at the number on the wall, which read 27 and shook her head.

"That's blood," Elliott confirmed. He turned to Aaron, and they both chuckled. "Damn that hurt, didn't it?"

"It didn't feel good," Jo's father admitted as they joined the other pair.

"You cut yourselves to write numbers on the tunnels?" Cadence shook her head. "I'm really glad I wasn't in here with you guys when all that was happening."

"Not that you were too happy being left out," Aaron reminded her. "The tunnels won't be in order now, so we may as well just start walking around looking for the luckiest number around."

"I'm sure Holland did that on purpose," Cadence mumbled as they walked to the next opening. They had to be careful when they stepped in front of it because Christian could be anywhere. Elliott was doing his best to stay between her parents and any imminent threat from the hub, and Jo had her weapon drawn and pointed across the expanse as everyone else looked at the numbers. She was quite certain her parents would be able to recognize the right number when they saw it.

And yet, she did find herself extremely distracted. She had no idea where Ryker and Jamie had rushed off to, but she imagined they wouldn't appear back in the hub until after they'd located Brandy. Then, they'd have to try to save her, if she could even be saved. Did Christian do something to her, or was it a monster attack?

And where the fuck was Zane? She let out a deep breath and willed her eyes to crawl down the tunnels. They were so dark, it wasn't possible to see all the way down any of them, but she could see the entryways. She would be able to see if Christian was standing near any of them.

If she saw the bastard, she'd shoot first and ask questions later.

A flicker of movement in one of the tunnels to their right had her spinning around, ready to fire. Elliott made himself as wide as possible, covering her parents, and her dad pushed him out of the way, not wanting his friend to take a bullet for him.

Elliott could die in here, too.

"It's us!" Lucy's voice hit her ear right before she pulled the trigger. The blonde stepped out of the tunnel timidly, her own weapon drawn. "Lucy and Scott!"

"Thank the good Lord," Elliott muttered. "Just us," he shouted back.

"Cadence, Aaron, Elliott, and Jo," Cadence supplied. "Are you guys okay?" Their party started moving in that direction with Jo insisting on going around the far side of her parents so that Elliott was on one side of them and she was on the other. Her mother kept trying to move past her, but Jo wasn't budging. The two of them deserved to live a long happy life together–even if it killed her.

"We're fine," Lucy answered as the two parties met up near the outer edge of the tunnel they'd emerged from. "Cadon, Cass and Brandon are taking the Vampire to tunnel thirteen right now so that we can get out of here. We're going to try to get the IACs back on."

"Where's everyone else?" Jo asked, not wanting to name names, though she was only thinking about Zane.

"Dax wasn't doing so good," Scott explained, shaking his head slightly. "I guess it was too difficult for him to be in here."

"You guys brought Dax in here?" Aaron's eyes widened in shock. "Whose stupid decision was that?"

"It was a… group decision," Elliott said, giving the impression it had been his idea.

"It was Brandon's," Scott clarified. "I don't think anyone expected him to react that way. Anyway, my mom and Zane took him out."

Jo's stomach dropped to her knees. On one hand, she was glad Zane wasn't in here anymore, that he was out of danger. On the other, well, he was obviously hurt and probably pissed at her. She'd have to wait until all of this was over to apologize and tell him she hadn't meant to hurt his feelings. She'd have to figure out a way to make things better.

Unless, of course, she didn't want to….

"Jo?" Her dad had obviously been speaking to her. "Are you all right?"

"Fine," she said with a nod. "Any idea where the IAC transmitter is?"

Aaron shook his head. "No. I just remember Christian telling me it was in the hub somewhere."

Lucy jumped in. "I saw some notes about it on Christian's computer. I know he tried to hide it so that the monsters didn't fuck with it, but I hope it'll stick out. I think he said he was hiding it near tunnel seventeen so he wouldn't forget it. What significance seventeen has to him, I have no idea."

"He was born in the seventeen hundreds," Aaron reminded them. "That's probably why."

"Okay. We'll find it and try to get things up and running again. Cadon should be somewhere around the opening to the place where the Vampires were keeping Cadence. He said he wanted to guard the entrance for some reason."

"We'll find him," Aaron assured her. "Elliott, you should go with Lucy and Scott. Even the numbers up."

"No fucking way," Elliott growled. "She's got a Healer with her. You don't."

"I'll be fine." Aaron's tone conveyed there would be no arguing.

Elliott doubled down. "Nope. Not happening."

"Elliott," Jo began, grabbing him by the shoulder. "It's fine. Go with them. My parents will be fine. I'll make sure of it."

His green eyes bore a hole through her skull. "I don't like this Lil Jo."

"I know you don't, but it'll be fine." She turned and looked at her father. "Cadon has your old watch. Maybe you should give your new one to Elliott so they're not both together?"

Without hesitation, Aaron slipped the watch off and stepped closer to his best friend, showing him how to use it.

Elliott managed to wedge it over his enormous hand. "I still don't like this."

"It'll be fine." Aaron slapped him on the shoulder, and the two parties split.

In the back of her mind, Jo had a bad feeling, but she couldn't second-guess herself now. Everyone would be fine and make it out of this alive. She had to believe that, even if the nagging voice in the back of her mind was saying otherwise.

25

Cadon

"I KNOW IT'S HERE SOMEWHERE," Cassidy said, walking back and forth down a particular part of the tunnel over and over again, searching for what she described as a glowing white light from the ground. Brandon was looking, too, while Cadon stood next to the Vampire, keeping guard, just in case one of the creatures tried to jump out at them. "Goddamnit."

"It'll appear," Brandon insisted. "We just have to keep looking. If it was easy to find, Aaron and Christian would've found it a long time ago."

"I know, but I actually know where to look for it. I'm sure it's between this chunk of black rock and that one over there," she said, still pacing.

Cadon let out a long breath trying not to sound bored. Neither of them seemed to notice. He kept checking his IAC, hoping it flickered to life soon. It would be nice to know where the rest of the team was. They'd killed a lot of monsters on their way over here, which was easy with his Aunt Cass around. She could throw shields and use her powers to blast the creatures away from them, throwing their bodies into the wall and what-not. But all he had to rely on at the moment was his weapon.

This was one of those tunnels that linked to the one next to it. A narrow passage joined this tunnel to what he guessed must be tunnel fourteen, though he wasn't sure. He didn't know how that worked when they spun and changed positions either. Could a person be in there when the tunnels repositioned and step out into a different tunnel than the one they'd entered from?

"I never should have suggested Dax come in here," Brandon lamented as the two of them continued to pace.

"You couldn't have known he'd react that way," his wife said with a reassuring tone.

"I should have." Brandon stopped moving for a moment, his eyes stuck in the same place on the ground, as if he'd found the magical opening, but then he shook his head and continued to search. "It's not like you handled it very well when you saw Alex."

Cassidy stopped her search and glared at him. "That was totally different."

"Not totally." Brandon tipped his head to the side. "It reminded him of Tara. I should've realized it would."

"Everything reminds him of Tara," Cassidy went back to her search, no longer giving her husband a death glare. "When you lose someone like that, it doesn't take much of anything to remind you of them."

It was quiet for a second before Brandon asked, "Are we still talking about Alex?"

Cassidy's body went rigid, and Cadon slowly shook his head. Such a bad move on his uncle's part.

"Fuck no," Cassidy turned around and met his gaze. "Are you shitting me?"

"Just wondering."

"I meant my sister, you asshat," she took a step forward, as if she was trying to get away from him. "Sometimes I think your head couldn't get any further up your ass than—"

Then, she was gone. There was a slight whooshing sound, totally different from the noise they heard when the portals opened, but noticeable, and Cassidy disappeared, right through the floor.

"Holy fucking shit!" Brandon exclaimed, shuffling over to where she'd dropped through the ground. "Cass? Can you hear me?"

There was no answer. Cadon stood up straight, on high alert now, wondering what they should do. Obviously, the Vampire was still over here.

Brandon dropped down on his knees, his gaze crawling across the craggily floor. "Cass? Cass?"

A hand shot up from the blackness, grabbing him by the throat. It was clearly his wife.

Without being able to speak, Brandon gestured at Cadon, making a beckoning motion with his hand. Cadon understood what he was getting at and grabbed the Vampire, handing him off to Brandon just in time for Cassidy to yank both of them through the hole—and with another whoosh, Cadon was left in the tunnel all alone.

"What the fuck?" he muttered, shaking his head.

It would be a bad idea to get too close to that hole. He knew that. Not only did he not want to accidentally fall down there, he didn't want anyone, or anything, to reach up and grab him. So he stayed a few feet away—far enough that nothing could grab him but close enough that he could shoot anything that tried to come out or go in.

The tunnels grew eerily quiet as he stood there by himself. Without his IAC, he felt completely alone in the world, which was something he hadn't experienced much. He decided it would be best to stay ready to shoot should any danger appear. The tunnels were dark, and it was quite possible for a demon or a demon hunter to show up out of nowhere.

And he had the other connecting tunnel to worry about, too.

Standing there, pacing, with his back mostly to one wall, his mind wandered. His dad was alive and back with them—that was good. He hoped it stayed that way. It wouldn't shock anyone if Christian decided to kill Aaron, should he get the chance. He wondered if Lucy and Scott had made it to the place where Christian had hidden the device that enabled their IACs to work. Obviously, it wasn't working yet, but maybe it would soon.

He thought about his parents, the fact that they were together again. Was his sister with them? She probably was.

What was the deal with Zane? Why had he been willing to leave? He knew he'd missed something in all the kerfuffle, but he had no idea what it was. Had the two of them had a fight?

He'd never been close to Jo. Actually, that wasn't true. When they were much younger, they'd been the best of friends. But then she'd learned how to talk and instantly become bossy.

When their mom was taken, he'd blamed his sister. She wasn't old enough to have done anything to prevent it. He knew that now, but at the time, he'd put himself in Jo's position. He would've done a better job of fighting the kidnappers off, or so he'd told himself.

When Jo had cussed their dad out and left the team, he'd been done with her. How dare she treat her family that way? What kind of a selfish bitch did a thing like that when they were in a crisis?

But there had definitely been times when she was in Nevada that he'd missed her. He'd hear stories about what she was doing out there, all the Vampires she was killing. She'd get arrested and manage to break out of jail. She'd even managed to get herself into Alcatraz a time or two to visit some of the prisoners and hadn't been forced to stay. She was out there living her life while he stayed back with the rest of the team, trying to make things work. Even their dad wasn't around most of the time. He was always in the tunnels. The team was spread all over the place, and Cadon spent a lot of his time in Canada with his grandparents—a grandpa who couldn't remember who anyone was and a grandma who just wanted her daughter back.

"Those were the days," he muttered.

Now that they were all back together again, would it be possible for his family to get along? Could he recreate that bond he'd had with Jo when they were little kids? He doubted it, but he did hope he'd have a chance to try. As long as she stayed put for a while, and no one died, he'd get another opportunity to have a sister like the ones he'd always read about in books and seen in movies.

For a split second, he thought he saw movement on the IAC and wondered if that meant Lucy had found the device. He stopped moving, his free hand crinkling in a fist, but then it faded away.

A noise to his left caught his attention, and he spun in that direction in time to see a large monster with fangs and sharp claws bearing down on him. Cadon fired several times, but the monster just kept coming. It was almost on top of him when gunfire rang out from a bit further down the tunnel. The monster skidded to a stop and toppled over, dead.

Cadon turned to see Jo rushing toward him. "Are you okay?"

He nodded. "Fine. Thanks. Wonder why…"

"Sometimes it's all about the angle with these things." She patted him sharply on the shoulder. "Don't ask me why. You stay in here long enough, you'll figure out all their tricks."

He wanted to say more, but then his parents came into view behind her. "Jo, I told you not to run off," Cadence scolded, but then she saw Cadon, and her face broke into a smile. She held up her hand, which was wrapped around Aaron's. "Surprise!"

Forgetting all about guarding the tunnel, Cadon rushed over to his parents and wrapped his arms around his father's neck. "You're back."

"I'm back, son." Aaron pounded him on the back, and Cadon had to blink back tears. He was so thankful that his dad had made it back from the other side, even if he'd never intended to make the journey.

"What are you doing exactly?" Jo asked behind him, interrupting the reunion.

"Making sure nothing comes in or out of that hole in the ground," he explained. "Cass and Brandon took the Vampire down there. They should be back soon."

Jo nodded and looked around. "The portal might open again any minute. I hate that we can't tell how much time has passed down here."

"I saw a flicker on my IAC," Cadon explained. "Did you guys?"

"A few seconds before the gunfire started?" Cadence asked. "Yeah. I think Lucy must have found the device."

Cadon nodded. "That's good. Hopefully, Scott can keep her safe while she gets it up and running."

"Scott and Elliott," Aaron corrected. He took a deep breath and looked around. Cadon knew he was calculating their next move. "We don't really all need to be standing here guarding this opening. I'm worried about Jamie, Ryker, and Brandy."

"Who?" Cadon asked, not recognizing the last name.

"The woman that killed Christian the first time," Jo explained. "She came through the portal with us."

"Oh." He felt like asking a lot of other questions at the moment wouldn't be the best idea.

"If you heard that scream a while ago, we think that was her," his mother explained. "We sent Jamie to find her to help her if he can, and Ryker went with him."

"Right." Cadon felt like he was almost up to speed, but not quite. At the mention of Ryker's name, Jo turned around quickly. "Was Ryker hurt earlier?"

"He's fine now," Aaron assured him, glancing at his daughter. "Maybe I should go look for the—"

"No!" the rest of the family yelled before the Guardian Leader could even get the full sentence out of his mouth.

"You are not going anywhere. Especially not alone." Cadence reached out and grabbed her husband by the shoulder.

"All right!" he lamented. "I just don't like having them off on their own, that's all."

"Jamie can heal anyone who gets hurt, including himself," Jo reminded them. "We should spread out. Is that a connecting tunnel?" She motioned to the area Cadon had been keeping an eye on the whole time.

"It is. You wanna take that, Jo?" Cadon asked.

Her eyebrows raised slightly, like she couldn't believe he'd taken the initiative to suggest anything. "Sure."

"I'm not leaving your father's side," Cadence declared.

"That's cool. I'll hang out over here by the opening," he said with a shrug.

"All right. We'll head closer to this end of the tunnel since it's further to the hub than the other end is." Aaron gave him a reassuring nod, and the two of them disappeared into the darkness.

Cadon took a deep breath. Nothing would be able to get to him now as long as the rest of his family kept their positions, unless it came from the far end of the tunnel, back toward the outer loop. With his back to everyone else, and the opening his aunt and uncle had disappeared down, he took up his position, ready to kill anything that moved.

26

Jo

DAMN, was she ready to get out of here and go home already. How much time had she spent in these fucking tunnels over the last few weeks? Too many hours to count. As Jo took up her position in the smaller tunnel that joined thirteen to whatever tunnel happened to be next to it at the moment, she kept both ears open. It seemed strange to her that Christian hadn't reared his ugly head recently. Sure, it was probably him who had made Brandy scream both times, but the fact that he hadn't snuck up on them or took a few shots at any of the team members seemed unusual to her.

Leaning back against the tunnel wall, Jo took a few slow deep breaths. She felt safe knowing she had her family behind her so she could concentrate all of her efforts toward what was happening in front of her.

At the moment, that wasn't much. No monsters skirted by through the tunnel she was staring into, and she heard nothing behind her.

It had been a relief to reach her brother in time to shoot that monster. She had a feeling he would've landed the money shot before it killed him, but it was getting kind of close. Jo shook her head. The fact that she could give tips on how to kill these fuckers told her she needed to get out of there and never come back.

Her mind wandered to Zane, and she let out a little sigh. What was she going to tell him? That she didn't mean what she'd said to Ryker? That she'd been lost in the heat of the moment? But was that the truth?

She honestly didn't know. It wasn't like she was married to Zane. But Ryker was the kind of guy that made her wish he was a Vampire most of the time so she could shoot him. They fought more than they got along. Zane had always been there for her, always been her soft place to fall–until she fucked it up.

And this wasn't the first time she'd done that either.

She knew how much he cared about her. Why did she have to be so fucking stupid? How could she forget about the little chip that had been in her eye for so long it was like a part of her?

Thinking about the IAC seemed to bring it to life for a second, though she was sure it was just a coincidence. It flickered a couple of times, giving her a bit of a visual she couldn't quite unscramble before it went dead again.

Jo's forehead scrunched as she tried to figure out what she'd been seeing. Was that Jamie kneeling over someone who was lying on the tunnel floor? The image had a hazy blue cast to it, which made her think it was one of the Healers, and it didn't seem to be out in the hub, which made her think Jamie was trying to heal someone.

But was it Brandy or Ryker?

Her stomach began to swim as she thought about the possibility of Ryker being injured again. Surely, Jamie and Ryker wouldn't have split up long enough for Ryker to get hurt, right?

She swore under her breath and reminded herself she needed to concentrate. With any luck, the IACs would be on again soon, and then they could get everyone together and get them out of there.

Another flicker brought her a different image. This time, she was sure she knew what she was looking at. It was Lucy working on the device with Scott next to her. She was looking through Lucy's IAC, so she could see a piece of metal jutting out of the rock near Scott's arm, but she couldn't see Elliott. The way that Lucy was quietly working on typing commands into the narrow screen made her think her "funcle" was just fine and probably standing behind her, ready to shoot anything that leaped out.

Still, it was just a flicker, and then it was gone. A sigh of frustration leaked from between her lips. They needed to get on with this and get the fuck out of there already before the demons came back or Christian showed up. She wasn't sure which would be worse.

A strange noise from the tunnel in front of her caught her attention. This place was full of weird noises, so it wasn't anything too alarming, but she didn't want to get caught off guard. It could be one of those damn demons, or maybe it was something else.

Jo moved as quietly as possible toward the entrance to the other tunnel and peered into the darkness. As far as she could see, she thought it was clear. Off in the distance, she thought she heard an eerie sound and leaned in a bit, straining to try to pick it up.

Whatever it was, the noise didn't seem to be originating within this tunnel. No, it was coming from her left, toward the outer loop, and probably at least three or four tunnels around the curve from where she stood. The urge to run to the end of the tunnel to investigate had her feet moving, but she didn't go far.

It was a high-pitched, soft noise, not like the whooshing sound the portal made when it opened. Light and airy, she could hardly discern it at all. It was like she was hearing the echo of an echo.

Her mind strained to identify what it was and where she recognized it from, but before she could get there, her IAC flickered to life again.

This time, it stayed on, at least, long enough for them to communicate. *"I've got it up,"* Lucy said, *"but some of the pieces are broken. We're going to have to stay here to keep it running."*

"Well done!" her mother said to the other team. Jo shifted her visuals so she could Cadence standing next to Aaron in the tunnel behind her. *"We knew you could do it, Lucy."*

"Ryker and I are in tunnel thirty-two. We found Brandy a few minutes ago. She was almost dead when we got here. I'm doing what I can to help her, but... it's not looking so good. Even for me." Jamie's tone sounded heavy and distracted as Jo clued in on what he was doing. Brandy lay on the ground in front of him, several slash marks across her throat, abdomen, and chest.

"Can you tell what happened?" Elliott asked.

"No, not really," Ryker responded, probably so that Jamie could continue his work. He was standing guard, looking back and forth down both sides of the tunnel. *"It's hard to say if it was a knife or claws."*

"I'd lean toward the former, though," Jamie said, his hands emanating that warm blue light that usually brought people right back from death.

Was he weaker in here for some reason? Jo had never seen him struggle like that before. Maybe Christian had used something on a knife he'd used to stab Brandy. But what?

Surely, he wouldn't have any scandium on him, would he? Would that even matter? He wasn't a Vampire, and Brandy wasn't a Guardian.

"Might be laced with titanium," Jamie muttered.

That made more sense. She let out a deep breath. If that was the case, Christian was definitely the one to blame for this, and if he could do that to Brandy, he could do the same to any of them.

She stood up a little taller and narrowed her eyes a little more, trying to see into the tunnels.

"We have the Vampire placed," Cassidy said. *"We're heading back toward the hole now."*

"Great. As soon as Cass and Brandon get here, we'll all meet back up at the hub and get the hell out of here." Cadence sounded like she was definitely the one in charge here, and Jo was glad for it. While she seriously hoped her parents got to take a long vacation after all of this, she didn't want to be in charge of anything at the moment.

It was kind of nice to take a step back and let someone else give the orders.

But she couldn't relax too much.

She switched her main visuals from one teammate to another. Jamie wasn't having any luck, and it was clear he was about to call it when a different IAC flickered to life in front of her very eyes.

Confused, Jo took a step backward, trying to make sense of what she was seeing. No name was assigned to the team member, and whoever it was seemed to be pulling themself up, slowly and silently, out of the hole in the ground that Cass and Brandon had passed through to drop the demon off.

She was very familiar with that fucking hole having gone through it to get her mom out.

It wasn't Brandon. It wasn't Cass….

When her brother's back came into view in front of her, Jo sucked in a shuddering breath. "Fucking Christian!" she whispered, spinning around.

But by then, it was too late. Everything was happening too quickly. The whoosh of the portal opening, the motion the madman made to grab her brother from behind, the rush of panic that shot right through her body as her mother screamed, also having put together what was going on.

She was only a few steps away from Christian as he lunged toward her unsuspecting brother over in tunnel thirteen, but with the portal opening, everything shifted, and being in a center tunnel meant Jo was about to get reshuffled herself. Even racing toward Cadon wouldn't guarantee she'd get there in time to do anything.

But it would give her away. Christian had to know where she was since his IAC was on, right?

She only had one chance to save her brother—to save her family. Making a quick decision, Jo switched her IAC off completely and sprinted in the other direction.

27

Cadon

THE HAIRS on the back of his head stood on end abruptly. Something had changed—something was off. Seeing nothing through the darkness in front of him, Cadon turned to check if perhaps a monster had somehow snuck up on him from behind.

It was a monster, all right, but not the kind he'd been suspecting.

Christian lunged at him while his back was mostly turned to the Guardian. With a rage clearly fueled by insanity, the major grabbed Cadon's Beretta and squeezed it against his chest as he pulled back on him. Caught off guard, there was little the Hunter could do to defend himself.

Especially when he realized Christian had a knife pressed against his throat.

"Toss it," he commanded, spittle coating Cadon's cheek. He threw the gun away as instructed, thinking he'd have to do something else to get out of this situation, but for now, he needed to comply. Christian's arm wrapped around his middle to hold him in place with the gun he'd been using for leverage lying on the side of the tunnel. A helpless feeling washed over him as Christian slowly turned him around.

Cadence and Aaron came running through the darkness, stopping short when they saw Christian had a knife to their son's throat. This was no steak knife either. Through his mom's IAC, Cadon could see the serrated blade on the six inch long weapon that pressed so tightly on his windpipe he was having difficulty sucking in a cigarette-smoke ladened breath.

"Christian," Aaron said calmly, raising his empty hands in front of his chest as a symbol of surrender. "Whatever you're planning to do, it's not necessary. Let Cadon go, and let's talk about this like old friends."

"Old friends?" A maniacal laugh echoed through the tunnels resounding in Cadon's left ear which was practically crushed against Christian's hairy cheek. He even looked like a lunatic, with his long beard and unkempt hair. "We have never been friends."

"That's not true." Aaron took a small step forward, but Christian yanked back on the knife without warning, slicing into Cadon's throat. A sliver of pain bit into his throat, but after the small wince that escaped his lips, he fought against acknowledging Christian at all. If he spoke up or tried to negotiate for himself, he'd likely just make the situation worse. It was best to let his parents do the talking while he tried to think of something else to do to free himself.

"I've always fucking hated you," Christian continued. "Since the day I first met you, I knew you were a conceited prick who got his jollies from ordering everyone else around."

"Christian, we worked together on some of the most important hunts in history," Aaron argued. "Dracula. Titanic. Holland. Daunator."

Christian shaking his head sent his whiskers rubbing against Cadon's cheek, which was unpleasant in so many ways. "No, you led those hunts, and I was just one of your fucking minions. You've tried to throw me off the team so many times, I can't even count them. Then, you finally died, and I had a chance at what I really wanted, and you didn't even have the decency to stay dead."

"What is it you really want, Christian?" Cadence asked. She still had her gun drawn, though it wasn't pointing directly at them. For some reason, Christian didn't seem threatened by it. Probably because his mother would have to shoot him in order to kill his assailant.

"Power." The one-word answer was enough, but then the Guardian elaborated. "I should've been the one to take over after Jordan died. God, to think I almost killed you off before the two of you even got married."

"The shot?" Aaron asked. "Well, that was my own stupidity."

"No, I like for you to think that, but believe me, there was more going on in the background there than you'll ever know." Christian laughed again, and the knife bit into his throat once more. Blood trickled down toward his collar. Cadon could feel the tickle as it dripped.

"What do you want now, Christian?" Cadence's tone had an edge of pleading to it. "You don't want to kill Cadon. He's never done anything to you."

"Ha!" Christian increased his grip. "Both of your asinine children have afflicted me grievously. Who knows what I might've been able to accomplish if you hadn't tied yourself to that scumbag with them."

"So this is about me?" Cadence asked. "I'm confused. Having me and having power are two different things."

"They are the same!" Christian screamed. Cadon closed his eyes as his ear began to ring. "You wield all the power. Having you is the ultimate power move."

"Killing my son isn't going to get you any closer to that," his mom reminded the lunatic.

"Oh, we're past that now, Cadence. You made your choice—time and again. You keep fucking choosing him, even when he's dead!"

"Christian, we had no intention of trying to bring Aaron back through the Blue Moon Portal." Cadence edged her way forward a step, but Christian stopped her with a grunt. "If you hadn't opened that portal into 'the beyond,' he would still be in there. Can you please tell me why you did that?"

"Why did I do that?" The Guardian snickered. "One word. Chaos."

His parents said nothing in response, but as Christian continued to ramble about his intentions, it became clearer to Cadon that he needed to do something. The rest of the team was lighting up the IAC with questions about what they should do to help. Lucy was afraid to let go of the device she was using to keep the IACs up, and she needed Elliott and Scott to keep her safe. Jamie had finally gotten a pulse on Brandy and didn't know if he should stay and keep helping her or go, and Cassidy and Brandon were moving as quickly as they could through the tunnel below his feet to try to help.

Where the fuck was Jo?

"My life had been upended so many times by you and your selfish actions, I wanted to make sure there was no peaceful life in eternity for you, you bastard," Christian explained. "Besides, who doesn't want to be the man who merged heaven and hell? But when the portal opened, I wasn't able to cross through myself. Only the demons could make it over. I had to stay here and hope that you'd be stupid enough to come through so I could kill you again. This time, it'll be a lot harder for you to be brought back since your body will be in here."

"Are you going to kill all of us then?" Cadence's tone was full of irritation now as she tired of dealing with a madman. "You don't think any of us would take him out?"

"You don't think Cassidy is about to blast through that hole in the floor and slam you into the ceiling?" Aaron had also lost his patience, clearly. "She's been wanting to kill you for a long time."

"Oh, I know I'm going to die." Christian spoke with a nonchalance that didn't match his words. "I've done it before. I'm not afraid to die."

"Your watch won't work in there," Aaron told him. "It won't open up a portal to let you back in here, if that's what you're thinking."

Christian chuckled. "Like you'd have the balls to try."

"You wouldn't remember or want to use it anyway," Cadence argued. "When you get to 'the beyond,' all of this will fade from memory, you know that."

"It didn't for you," Christian reminded her.

"That's because Jamie hit me with his light before I died. And because of the babies. Are you fucking pregnant, Christian?" Cadence asked, raising her weapon enough to catch his attention.

"You need to go ahead and put that down," Christian said. "Toss it."

His mother hesitated, locking eyes with Cadon. Through the IAC, he told her, *It's okay, Mom. We'll be all right. Cass is almost here.* He wished that was true, but the tunnel beneath them was a long one, and he couldn't tell where his aunt was at the moment.

Reluctantly, Cadence tossed her gun away. "Christian, we're not getting anywhere. What do you want? What's your plan? If I agree to go with you, wherever you're going, will you let my son go?"

"Fuck no," the lunatic answered quickly. "I don't want you anymore. Brandy's going to be waiting for me on the other side."

"Actually, if you check your IAC, she's not," Cadence said. "She's alive."

"No, I cut her up real good. With titanium. Same shit that's on this knife. Besides, the IACs aren't working. I shut that down." He shook his head, and the knife bit deeper into Cadon's flesh.

"The IACs are working. Lucy got them up and running. We can even see yours," Cadence argued. "Brandy's alive."

Christian pulled his head back slightly before he shook it again. "Shut the fuck up. That's not true."

"Why do you think Jamie's not here?" Aaron asked.

"Because he's fucking lost," Christian argued. "I should hope no one is stupid enough to try to sneak up on me. I have eyes in the back of my head. I'll kill them before they can lift their weapon."

"Are you sure about that?" Aaron chided. "They'd just have to be smarter and faster than you, and that's not saying much."

Grunting, Christian said, "You're such a fucking prick. I can't wait to paint the tunnels red with your blood."

If he can't track us, then sneaking up on him is our best bet, Ryker said through the IAC, obviously willing to chance Christian's threat of certain annihilation.

Go, Jamie told him.

"You can't beat all of us, Christian. I'm aiming for your head first and then that watch," Cadence taunted.

Christian seemed to realize the tides may be changing. When he spoke again, his tone was tinged with panic. "This is going to end with the three of you dead and me opening a portal back to LIGHTS," he explained.

"No, it's not. Like you just said, this is going to end with you dead. How many of us you take with you remains to be seen, but you're not walking out of here," Aaron assured him.

"You hurt Cadon, I kill you," Cadence said through gritted teeth. "You shoot Aaron, I kill you. You shoot me–"

"I rip your fucking head off before she hits the ground," Aaron finished.

Christian pressed the knife harder against Cadon's throat and let go with his other arm for a split second. Cadon contemplated making a move, but the pressure on his throat was too great, and a second later, Christian's other arm was back, but this time, he was holding a Glock. "You can't actually think I'm not going to shoot you first, right, Aaron?"

"Well, if that's the case, what the fuck are you waiting for?" Aaron spread his arms wide as if he was welcoming some sort of resolution to the conflict.

"No!" Cadence moved between them. "You have to shoot me first, and I don't think you want to do that, Christian. You told me you loved me once, remember?"

Christian shrugged. "I lied. That's what I do."

Cadon felt Christian's trigger finger flinch and knew it had all finally come to a head. As Christian fired his first round, Cadon rammed his elbow straight back into his captor's chest, feeling the knife slice across his throat as he tried to duck out of the way.

Multiple gunshots rang out, so many he couldn't tell where most of them were coming from as he rocketed forward across the tunnel floor, propelled from some unknown force from behind, hitting the ground hard and rolling several feet.

Breathing was impossible as blinding pain shot through his entire body. He reached for his throat, willing the blood to stop pouring down his neck and the back of his throat, but his feeble fingers did nothing to shore up the dam as every inhale gurgled in his throat.

He was going to die.

28

Jo

EIGHT MINUTES EARLIER...

NAVIGATING the tunnels after the spin was difficult. She'd made it into the adjoining tunnel just as the portal had opened. She'd booked it toward the back of that path toward the outer loop, hoping she didn't run into any demons on the way. She wouldn't be able to open fire on anything without letting Christian know something was up.

As it was, she didn't have any idea how she was going to manage to pull this off. How many times had she seen Christian shoot a creature in one of these tunnels before anyone else even knew it was there? He had some sort of a fucking sixth sense. If she could distract him enough, maybe her parents would be able to take a shot from the other direction and get her brother to safety. That's all she needed.

As she sprinted around the outer loop, listening for voices to clue her in as to which tunnel Christian's hostage situation was playing out in, she came to the conclusion that she was about to die. The realization washed over her with a level of acceptance she'd never really thought she'd experience. But the only alternative she had to putting herself in harm's way was to hang back and let someone else solve the problem. She couldn't let either of her parents die, and she would never forgive herself if her twin brother died, so she had to face facts.

Not everyone was walking out of there alive.

Christian had to die, though. She had to shoot him and make sure he didn't get through a portal. If he managed to open a wormhole and get through it back to the real world before he died, he simply wouldn't die.

No, letting him escape also wasn't an option.

Hearing voices in the distance, Jo slowed. Sounds echoed off the tunnel walls making strange reverberations which didn't always make it easy to recognize who was talking or what they were saying. She realized now that the noise she'd heard before was Christian whistling. He had to have been scouting out their position before he opened a portal beneath where Cadon was standing and used the other level of tunnels to sneak up on him. If he'd opened a portal right where her brother was standing, he would've heard that, but going through that weird glowing opening was noiseless.

Which was exactly what she needed to be at the moment.

This was it. Tunnel thirteen. She'd found it. She could hear Christian laughing and the sound of her father's voice as she began to pick her way through the darkness. Thankfully, all the demons seemed to be elsewhere at the moment, which might just give her the one chance she needed to kill Christian. How many times had she asked herself if he had some sort of influence over them? If he did, he needed to send them after her now.

It was nearly impossible to keep her boots from crunching over the tunnel floor because of the rocky surface. She couldn't rush this. Being methodical might just save her brother's life.

After about a hundred silent paces, Christian's form came into view in front of her. He was holding Cadon against his chest, and from her calculations, the opening to the shaft was about a step in front of them. He didn't seem to know she was there, and she needed to keep it that way. It would be easy to blow his fucking head off at this angle, but he might jerk that knife back and slice her brother's throat. She needed a better angle, so she slid up a few steps and to the left waiting to see if he flinched. If he knew she was there, he was the best bluff she'd ever seen.

She got into position just in time to hear her father issue an ultimatum and knew all hell was about to break loose. With no more time to weigh her options, Jo unleashed, firing at Christian as many times as she could pull the trigger.

He fired, and ducked to his right, yanking the knife as he went. He turned toward her and fired over his left shoulder as Jo left the ground, closing the distance between them in an instant.

Pain spread through her chest taking her breath away. He'd definitely landed a few shots, but then, she had, too. Adrenaline continued to course through her body as she tackled him. Christian let go of Cadon as he and Jo both began to fall.

But it wasn't to the ground on the top level of the portal. Instead, they fell straight through to the second level, Christian landing on bottom and taking the brunt of the force. Even though she could hardly suck in a breath because of the pain in her chest, Jo couldn't give up now. She was so close to ending this fucker once and for all.

With her left hand, she reached for his wrist, noting he was grappling to try to reach it, too. But he was bleeding profusely from the neck and shoulder, and the fall had knocked a lot out of him. Jo's right hand was pinned beneath Christian's back, but her left hand was free. She reached for his flailing left wrist, where he still held the blood soaked knife he'd used to slit her brother's throat, and worked a finger under the band of his watch, yanking it off him, flinging it against the tunnel wall, hopefully hard enough for it to break.

"Fucking bitch!" Christian yelled. He'd dropped his gun to try to activate his watch and was going for it now. Seeing it lying next to her knee, Jo couldn't let go of his wrist that held the knife to prevent him from reaching for the gun, so she used her knee to swipe it out of the way.

Her change in position gave him just enough leverage to work himself free, and as she attempted to pull her gun from behind him, he broke his wrist free of her grasp.

Jo watched in slow motion as the tip of the knife disappeared into her chest, right above her left breast. That maniacal cackle she hated so much filled her ears as the blade disappeared into her chest.

He was still laughing when she climbed off him and slid back against the wall of the tunnel. It was just a matter of time now. She was going to die–and so was he. Looking down at the handle protruding through her chest, Jo stared in disbelief. It didn't even really hurt that much.

She still had her weapon in her hand. She could blow his brain's out, but at this angle, she could see she'd hit him enough times before they'd fallen that he only had a few minutes at best himself.

"Well, I didn't get your dad, but I got both of you. That's... that's something." Christian collapsed onto the floor, a satisfied grin on his face.

"Yes, you should be quite proud." She wrapped her blood coated fingers around the handle and contemplated yanking it out, but that would probably just make her bleed out faster. She flicked on her IAC to see her brother bathed in blue light, though she couldn't tell if it was Jamie or Scott who had gotten there. A smile crept into place, and she began to laugh as well.

"Wh-what's so fucking funny?" Christian managed. "You... losin' it McReynolds?"

"Nope. It's just... my brother's gonna be just fine, you asshole."

He attempted to lift her head to look at her but couldn't. It slammed back into the floor. "No. I slit his fucking throat."

"Joke's on you. See you in hell, Henry." Deciding she'd had enough, Jo tried to lift her Glock to put him out of her misery, but a roaring sound from deeper in the tunnel followed by a blinding light told her that wouldn't be necessary.

Cassidy came roaring into view as the light reached Christian and picked him up off the ground. He hung in the air near the tunnel ceiling long enough to turn his head and meet Jo's eyes. Then, in an explosion loud enough to make her ears ring, Cassidy used her powers to rip him into a thousand pieces. Somehow, her aunt managed to keep the debris from landing on her.

Christian Henry had gotten exactly what he deserved.

Deciding she could live–and die–with that, Jo closed her eyes.

"Jo! Jo!" Cassidy cried. She felt hands on her jacket, thought she heard Brandon ask if she was breathing. In her IAC, she saw her father through her mother's IAC and realized he was dropping through to the tunnel where she was. Good. It would be nice that he could sit with her while she died, as she had done for him.

"We have to open the portal," Aaron was saying. "Scott's not strong enough, and Jamie's with Cadon."

The idea that she could still say something through the IAC crept to mind, but what was there to say, really? The people she loved knew it, and those who didn't wouldn't need to hear it now. The pictures coming through the IAC began to mesh together and scramble, and then, they were gone.

29

Cadon

"Breathe, baby. Breathe."

The sound of his mother's voice registered in Cadon's head as he slowly opened his eyes. Darkness surrounded him, other than the soft glow of Jamie's hands. He was still in the tunnels, but the Healer was there.

Tentatively, Cadon began to think perhaps he wasn't about to die.

"That's it. You're okay." Cadence's grip on his arm was almost as uncomfortable as the tightness he felt in his throat. The intense pain had faded into a dull throb, and when he sucked in a deep breath, the sound of gurgling that would likely haunt his dreams for all of eternity was gone.

"He's going to be okay," Jamie said, talking to his mother and anyone else who had gathered around him. He couldn't turn his head to look, but he sensed there were others nearby, and his IAC hadn't come back online yet. "He's stable enough for us to get him out of here now."

"Elliott's on his way with Aaron's watch," Cadence said.

"I-I have it," Cadon muttered, confused.

"Your dad took the one you were wearing to help Jo, honey," Cadence explained, still swiping at tears. "They needed to get her out of here and back to Cale."

"Wh-why?" Instinctively, he tried to sit up, but Jamie pressed him down.

"Fuck!"

That was Ryker, whom Cadon couldn't see at the moment, but he recognized his voice.

"You did everything you could," Jamie said, looking over his shoulder.

"It wasn't enough," Ryker said before the sound of crumbling indicated he'd kicked the wall--hard.

He could boot his IAC up and see if that would give him any clues, but instead, Cadon looked at his mother's face and knew that whatever had happened to his sister, it was bad. "Mom?"

"She, uh, she got stabbed, honey," Cadence replied, wiping her cheeks again. "And shot. It doesn't look good."

Still confused, Cadon tried to puzzle through his last memories. Christian had opened fire on his parents. He'd seen his dad push his mom out of the way, but he hadn't seen whether or not his dad had gotten shot again because he'd been too busy trying to disrupt Christian. After his throat had been slashed, he'd gone flying onto the ground. He had no idea why.

"Did she—" he began, but Jamie interrupted.

"She snuck up on Christian and opened fire when he shot at your parents. She pushed you both to try to disrupt Christian, and they both fell down to the bottom level. Cassidy said he stabbed her. Her IAC wasn't on until it was all over, so we didn't see any of that. Cassidy blew Christian to smithereens. Your dad took his old watch and went down there to get Jo to Cale."

Cadence broke into sobs, and Cadon decided he was healed enough. He pushed up again, and this time, Jamie let him sit. Wrapping his arms around his mom, he said, "She'll be okay, Mom. I'm sure of it."

"I hope so," Jo sobbed. "I can't imagine losing either one of you, not when we finally have the chance to be together as a family."

He held her against his shoulder and fought his own tears. He'd always thought his sister hated him, but she'd made the ultimate sacrifice to try to save him, and while he'd still gotten slashed, he was alive–and she might not be.

"I got here in time to save you, but we didn't know if I'd be able to get to her fast enough. That knife was coated with titanium, which has proven to make it harder to combat once it hits our systems, sort of like the titanium bullets that allow one Hunter to kill another Hunter," Jamie explained, answering his unspoken question of how had their parents chosen to put the strongest Healer on him instead of his sister.

Approaching footsteps alerted them that the rest of the team had arrived. He turned his head just as Scott, his best friend in the world, dropped to his knees and wrapped his arms around both him and his mom. "Thank god you're okay," Scott said.

"I'm all right," Cadon assured him.

"Nice to see you, Cade," Elliott said, ruffling his hair like he was a child. Lucy leaned down and gave him a quick squeeze as well. "Who wants to open this portal?"

"You do," Jamie replied. "Didn't Aaron show you how?"

"You know I'll fuck it up." The burly Guardian handed the watch to Jamie who took it and shook his head. "We should probably hurry up. Cale might need your help."

With a grim shake of his head, Jamie said, "If Cale needs my help, then it's already too late. Can you help Brandy?"

"I'm fine," a woman Cadon had never met said behind him as Scott helped him to his feet and Jamie offered Cadence a hand. He turned to look at her. Brandy was standing a few feet behind him, her clothes covered in blood, and a solemn look on her face. She'd been stabbed by a man who proclaimed to love her. Cadon didn't know her motivation for coming through the tunnels, but he had to imagine it wasn't for this.

Elliott messed around with the watch for a few seconds, and eventually, the portal opened. "I'll go last, just in case," he said.

"Cass placed the Vampire," Cadence reminded them. "It should be fine."

"Nevertheless…." Elliott gestured for them to all walk through the portal ahead of them, and with his mom's arm looped around his shoulders, Cadon stepped through.

It took a few moments to traverse the wormhole, but on the other side, they stepped out into Christian's office and a flurry of activity. Cadence and Jamie rushed over to Jamie's office where they could hear Cale and Martin shouting at one another in an effort to orchestrate what sounded like either resuscitation or emergency surgery. He couldn't be sure. Cadon waited by the portal opening for Elliott to step through, and when he did, he watched with satisfaction when the portal vanished.

"May we never have to go through there again," Lucy said.

"Amen," Elliott agreed.

Cadon rushed out into the hallway where a large group had gathered outside of the room where now three Healers were working on his sister. His parents were both in there as well. Ryker stood with his nose practically pressed to the glass, a place where Cadon would've been most comfortable.

"You should be in there," Elliott said, nudging him in the shoulder.

"There are already so many people around her, though." Something about standing there helpless watching his sister die, or watching the doctors try to bring her back, didn't seem appealing to him at all.

"Go on." Elliott hit him with his shoulder again. "You'll regret it if you don't."

"Cadon!"

Mallory's voice reached him from the end of the hallway as she came flying through the door. He turned and rushed toward her, taking her in his arms and breathing her in.

She pressed herself to his chest but then pulled back. "Oh, god!"

He looked down and remembered that he was absolutely coated with blood. It was now smeared on the side of her face. "I'm so sorry."

"You're sorry? Are you okay?" she blurted, her eyes searching every part of him she could see for an explanation for why he had so much blood on the outside of his body. "I heard you were back, and that your sister was hurt, but are you?"

"I was, but I'm fine now." He was certain he had to have blood all over his neck as well. He wondered if he'd have a scar.

She nodded in understanding, though he assumed she'd want to hear what happened later. "Where's Jo?"

"She's in Jamie's office," he said, shaking his head. "It doesn't look good."

"Shouldn't you be in there?" she asked, her voice a soft whisper.

He took a deep breath. "Yeah."

Mallory nodded. "I'll go with you, if you want."

Somehow, the idea of having her there with him made the unbearable seem slightly possible. He laced his fingers through hers and headed back toward the door. Squeezing past Ryker, they went inside.

Cadon kept his distance, letting the doctors work. His parents stood off to the side, his father's arms wrapped tightly around his mom who was weeping quietly. Both of them were absolutely covered in blood, and Aaron was favoring his shoulder. Had Christian managed to land that shot, and his dad was just suffering through it so that the Healers could concentrate on Jo? Scott was literally standing in the hallway and could've helped, but then, knowing his dad, he probably didn't even feel it; he was obviously extremely worried about Jo.

"We have to treat this like any other stab wound to a human being," Jamie was saying. "We're not going to get her back this way."

"We need blood," Cale called as the three of them scurried around doing who knew what. The Healer lifted his head and met Cadon's eyes. "Perfect match."

Without question, Cadon stepped forward. "Of course. What do you need?"

"Take off your jacket and roll up your sleeve," Martin told him, taking what was probably the easiest task as Jamie and Cale called to one another about CCs and oxygen levels and all other kinds of things he couldn't decipher. Mallory brought him a chair, and within minutes, blood was flowing out of Cadon again, but this time it was at a controlled pace and going directly into his sister.

"Does this mean she's still alive?" he asked, praying they wouldn't be going to all of this trouble if she wasn't.

"Something strange is happening," Jamie explained. "Her body has completely shut down from blood loss, but she still has brain activity."

"She was alive when they brought her in," Cale said from his position at Jo's head. "Her heart stopped beating about the time I hit her with my light. We're hoping that means she can come back, like your mom did."

"We're not going to give up," Jamie assured him. "We've got the wounds closed. We'll keep working to get her heart restarted."

Cadon nodded in understanding, but he was still confused. The monitors showed no pulse, no activity whatsoever with his twin's heart.

So why could he hear a faint heartbeat?

30

Jo

"Back so soon?"

The feel of plush grass beneath her hands had Jo gasping and sitting up. "Wh-what the fuck?"

"Now, now, Josephine, I told you earlier not to use that kind of language here," Janette said, wagging her finger. "Well, come on. You can't just sit in the grass all day. We have a lot to do."

Jo climbed to her feet and stared at the blue sky that seemed to stretch on forever. The field of velvety green grass rippled in the breeze, and a sense of peace settled over her.

She'd been here before. She knew that much. And Janette was her great-grandmother. She knew that, too. But that was all she could remember. Maybe the older woman could clue her into the parts she couldn't remember.

The two of them walked toward the main street where all the townsfolk were busy fixing what appeared to be extensive damage. "What happened?" she asked.

"Monsters. But they're all gone now." Janette smiled. "Never happened before. Hope it won't happen again."

Somehow, she vaguely remembered something about monsters, but she couldn't piece it together. "Was I here?"

"You were here, and then you were gone."

"But… did I fight the monsters?"

Janette turned and smiled at her. "We don't worry about the past here. When you're here, here is all that matters. Now, come help us put the roof back on the general store." She started walking again. "We could just wave our hands and fix it, but where's the fun in that?"

Jo laughed and headed over to where some people she thought she recognized were replacing a window in another shop. "That's right. That's perfect," a man dressed in a Revolutionary War uniform said, directing to other people where to install the glass. "Let's nail it in."

"Need a hand?" she asked, grabbing a hammer.

"That would be great–Jo." He smiled at her, and she suddenly knew his name was Alexander, though she wasn't sure how. "How are you?"

"Never better." She took a nail and held it against the wood frame, lining up the hammer and taking aim. For a moment, a flash of aiming at something else filled her mind. She shook her head to clear her thoughts and continued to hammer.

"I can help, too."

A familiar voice pulled her away from her work, and she turned to see a tall man with dirty blond hair picking up a hammer. His face was clean shaven, and he was wearing jeans and a cowboy shirt.

The scent of cigarette smoke tinged the air.

"Thank you, Christian. Nice to have you here." Alexander patted his back as the other newcomer began to strike his nail.

"Christian?" Jo repeated. "Do I know you?"

"I think so," he replied. "You're Jo, right? You just got here?"

"I guess," she said with a shrug. "I don't really remember where I was before I woke up in that patch of grass over there."

"Same," he said. "Weird." He went back to hammering and started whistling a song that also seemed vaguely familiar. Something about pirates.

Shaking her head, she went back to work. It was frustrating not being able to remember where she had been right before this, but everyone was so nice here. She just had the feeling that this was where she belonged.

A friendly-looking woman with a wide smile dressed in a long gown passed by on the sidewalk, holding the hand of a little girl with pale white skin and dark hair. "Look, Mama. They're fixing the window."

"That's right, Bonnie. They are." The woman smiled at Jo, and she nodded her head, following along as the pair passed them.

"That's Mina and her daughter," Alexander explained. "Nice folks."

"They seem like it." Jo watched them for a second, a nagging feeling growing in the pit of her stomach. "Do you have children, Alexander?"

"I do." He smiled proudly. "Eight of them, in fact. What about you, Jo? Do you have any children?"

"Yes," she said with a nod. "I have…." But then she stopped. No, that wasn't right. She didn't have any kids. She'd never wanted any–had she? "Wait. No, I guess I don't."

"Oh." Alexander shrugged. "That's too bad. Maybe you shall someday."

"Maybe."

She tried to go back to fixing the window, but the appearance of the woman with the little girl had her feeling like something was off. "Will you excuse me?"

"Of course. Are you well?" Alexander asked.

Setting down her hammer, Jo said, "I'm fine. Just a little off." She gave him a reassuring smile and then wandered a few steps away to a bench. While the townsfolk continued to go about their day, the nagging feeling that she was missing something settled even deeper. Jo placed her hands on her stomach.

"Are you all right?" a soft voice called.

Jo looked up to see a beautiful woman with long blonde hair and bright red lips hovering over her. "Ashley?"

"No, my name is Ellie," she said. "I'm afraid I don't know Ashley. Is that a friend of yours?" She sat down on the bench next to Jo.

Confused again, Jo shook her head. "No. I, uh, I mean… I don't know." Who was Ashley?

"You're new here, right? Sometimes it's easy to be confused when you first get here, but soon enough, that will all go away, and you'll settle in fine." She rested her hand on Jo's arm.

"Thank you. Everyone here is so nice and helpful. I just can't help but think… I'm missing something. I saw that woman with her little girl. I don't think I have kids. Do you?"

"No," Ellie said with a smile. "But that's okay. I have a mom and dad. They're over helping at the general store. Where are your parents?"

Parents? Did she have those? "I don't know," Jo admitted. "My great-grandmother is over there. I guess that means I have to have parents."

Shrugging, Ellie said, "Maybe not. Not everyone does. Well, if you need anything, just holler." She patted her arm again and then got up and practically skipped away.

"This isn't right," Jo murmured. She stood up and started walking back toward the grass where she had sat up only a few moments before. Something had been happening to her before she was here. She realized she was clutching her stomach. Had something been wrong there? Had she been hurt?

"No, that's not it." She stopped in the field of green and looked up at the sky. Janette had said she'd been here before. She had been–she'd fallen from the sky.

Why?

And why was she here now?

"Increase her oxygen level. Push twenty more CCs of epinephrine."

Jo looked around. Where was that voice coming from? It seemed to be coming from inside her head.

"That's too much," another voice said. *"Jamie–"*

"Just do it! We're losing her anyway!"

"Jamie?" she whispered, searching her mind for any reference to who that might be.

"I've got a sinus! It's weak, but it's there."

"Start compressions again. Let's try the defib. On my count, Cale."

"Cale?" Jo closed her eyes and reached out with her mind. Somehow, she could hear these voices, these people, and they were trying to fix something that was broken.

Something that had shattered.

Her eyes flew open. "Me. They're trying to fix me."

Jo spun around and looked at the town in the distance. She was in 'the beyond' but she wasn't meant to be there–not again. Not yet.

A flood of memories whooshed over her, knocking her backward onto the grass.

Her mother's face smiling down at her. Her brother laughing as a little baby. Her dad pouring her a bowl of cereal. A dog licking her aunt. Uncle Elliott tossing her up in the air. Jamie mending a scratch on her knee. Holding hands with Scott on their way to the pizza place. A walk with her mom in the woods. So much blood! Shouting at her father, cussing him out, running out the door. Riding a motorcycle through the desert. The echo of gunfire. Ash and smoke. Zane looking down at her with love in his eyes. Holland firing a shot at her dad. His face as he faded away. Wrapping her arms around her mother's shoulders in a tunnel full of white light. Falling from the sky. Looking down in horror to see a knife protruding from her chest. A tiny flicker on a screen fighting for life.

The soft grass beneath her hands faded away, and all was still and quiet until Jo dropped out of the sky again. This time, her eyes flew open, and she sucked in a deep breath through the mask on her face. Beeping and shouting created a cacophony, waves of blue light perpetuating the chaos as she stared up at a bright light.

"She's back! We've got her back!"

Jamie. That was Jamie. She remembered him.

His face came into focus above her. "Stay with us Jo. You're going to be all right." She tried to nod, but nothing happened. Out of the corner of her eye, she could see Cale and Martin step into frame as they worked on her. The more the light soaked into her body, the better she felt until she could hear with her own ears that her heart-beat was strong and steady.

"Thank God. Oh, thank God." Her mom's voice sounded close by, but she couldn't look at her at the moment.

Her IAC. That would help. She turned it on and immediately took in the scene around her through Jamie's IAC as he continued to use his powers to heal her. Her parents stood at the head of her bed out of the way, and her brother was seated next to her with some sort of tube in his arm. He was fine.

She took a deep breath and closed her eyes for a moment. She'd died–but she was alive now. She had no idea how it had happened, but she was back.

And Christian was dead.

"I'm okay," she whispered. Then, reaching up to wrap her fingers around Jamie's wrist, she said, "Jamie… I'm okay."

He blinked and nodded. "We're good. Cale, Martin, thank you."

Jo leaned up on her elbows as Jamie took the oxygen mask off. "Thank you–all of you." She locked eyes with her brother. "Thanks, Cadon."

"Thank you," he said. Cale removed the tape on his arm and pulled out the IV. He'd been giving her blood, apparently. "You saved me."

She smiled and reached for his hand, which he gave to her. "We saved each other."

Her parents were on her in a millisecond once they had permission to hug her from the Healers. Her mom's tears soaked her shoulder. "We thought we'd lost you."

"You did," Jo murmured.

"We're glad you're back, Jo." Her dad kissed the top of her head.

"Now, will you let me patch up your shoulder?" Jamie asked, tugging on the sleeve of Aaron's leather jacket.

"What's wrong with your shoulder?" Jo asked.

"It's just a flesh wound," he said with a crooked grin.

"Did you get shot?" She shook her head as Jamie dragged him a few steps away and fixed him.

"Only your father would stand there with a bullet wound in his shoulder for an hour without saying a word." Cadence sighed, but she was smiling. "You should be able to come home soon. Finally, we'll all be together under the same roof."

"Yeah, finally." That did make Jo happy. Except... there was someone missing. "Where's Zane?"

Cadence looked around, too, like she hadn't even thought about the man since she'd stepped through the portal.

"Who are you looking for?" Cale asked, wrapping up a cord that had likely been connected to her a moment ago.

"Zane," Cadence replied. "Is he out in the hallway with everyone else?"

"Oh, no. He… left," Cale said, his mouth turning down in a frown as he realized he was giving bad news to someone who'd recently died. "As soon as he got back from the portal, he packed up."

"Are you sure?" Cadence folded her arms across her chest. "Why would he do that?"

Cale shrugged. "I don't know. I asked him if he was all right, and he said he was fine, but he had some stuff to take care of back home. I'm sorry. I didn't realize–"

"It's fine, Cale. Thank you." Jo managed a smile, but she didn't feel it.

He'd left. And she couldn't blame him.

"There are a ton of people waiting out there to see you, Jo," Jamie said, once Aaron was all patched up. "But I need to talk to you alone for a few seconds first before we let you go."

"Is everything okay?" Her mother's forehead puckered in concern.

Jamie smiled at her. "Nothing to worry about. Could everyone go wait outside for just a quick minute?"

At the Healer's insistence, everyone left the room, though Cadence snuck in a quick kiss on Jo's forehead. They paraded out the door like the cast of a horror movie, covered in blood and grime. She looked down and saw that at some point someone had put her in a hospital gown, so at least she wasn't wearing her bloody clothes anymore, but she was covered in it, too, and needed a shower.

She figured Jamie just wanted to tell her how close she'd been to being gone for good, but when he stood in front of her with a serious expression on his face, she knew something was up. "What's going on?"

"On a day like this, there's no reason to beat around the bush. You're pregnant."

Instinctively, Jo covered her abdomen with both arms. "What? No. We always use condoms." Well, they usually did.

He shrugged. "Sometimes those don't work. I picked up on it when you were gone. We kept hearing a heartbeat. I ran the ultrasound when your folks were concentrating on what Cale was doing with the oxygen so they wouldn't notice. You're about four weeks, so not really long enough for you to detect it yet."

The ability to speak seemed to have left her. Jo nodded. "Okay. Thank you."

He patted her leg. "If you need anything–vitamins, nausea medicine, other help… let me know."

"Yeah. Okay."

"I won't tell anyone. Do you need a minute before I let the crowd back in? I can stand here and pretend to talk to you so you can process." He placed a reassuring hand on her shoulder.

"That would be great. Thanks." Jo closed her eyes and took a few deep breaths.

She remembered being in 'the beyond' and thinking she was missing someone–a child. She'd seen that woman walk by with her little girl–what was her name? Betty? Bobby?

"Bonnie," she whispered.

"What's that?" Jamie's forehead crinkled, but it wasn't a look of confusion. The way he leaned toward her, eyes wide, he looked alarmed.

"Oh, nothing. I was just thinking about something that I saw when I was dead. I'll let my parents know in a day or two, but I want to try to reach Zane first." She took a few deep breaths and put the news to the back of her mind–for now.

"Of course." Jamie patted her shoulder, but that wasn't enough, not even for Jo who didn't like to be touched.

She wrapped her arms around him and hugged him tight. "Thank you, Jamie. For everything."

"I love you, kiddo. Like you were my own," he said. "I'm just glad we were able to get you back." He stood up and smiled. "We've still got work to do."

"Don't I know it." She returned the smile and braced herself for the onslaught of people who would be pouring through that door when he opened it. Having friends was nice, but she was tired and had a lot on her mind. At least two Vampires probably came through when the portal opened. They'd need to find them.

Excited friends came rushing through the door. Her family hung back to let the people who hadn't gotten a chance to hug her do so first. Jo hugged Lucy, Elliott, Cass, Brandon, and a dozen other people before she looked up to see Ryker standing in front of her.

"Glad you didn't die," he said with that cocky grin on his face.

"Me, too."

He patted her shoulder and walked away, leaving her even more confused than she had been before—and that was saying something.

Eventually, she found herself back at home. After a shower, she put on a pair of pajamas and climbed into bed, thankful that her entire family would be sleeping in the same apartment for the first time in over ten years.

Noises from her parents' bedroom had her scrunching up her nose and putting on headphones. Maybe it was time to get her own place.

Jo turned up the music and reached for sleep, hoping she would at least see Zane in her dreams. She'd need to find him and tell him about the baby. It might not be enough for him to give her a second chance, but he needed to know.

She would need his help, not just raising a child, something she didn't want to think about, but hunting down the Demonic Vampires. They were out there somewhere, and she was coming for them, packing heat—and a baby.

EPILOGUE

"Mama?"

The little girl looked around the dark forest, taking in the sounds of creatures bounding around the tops of the trees and the fluttering of night birds crisscrossing the sky. She folded her arms across her chest and took a few tentative steps. The moon hung full above her head, illuminating her way as she began her search. In the distance, she saw what she presumed to be lantern light and began to walk that way.

Leaves crunched beneath her black patent leather shoes. Her frilly socks quickly became spattered with mud. Mama wouldn't like it if she got her dress dirty.

After an hour or two, she approached a house set off alone in the woods. The scent of woodsmoke poured from the chimney. Lights shone brightly from the windows. If Mama wasn't here, she'd continue toward the lights she'd seen from a distance, the lights of a village or small town.

Mama had to be here somewhere.

"Mama?" she called, standing beneath a large tree in the back of the house. "Mama?"

Where was she? Why wasn't she coming to help her? Sorrow filled her, and her tiny shoulders began to tremble as she pictured Mama's face in her mind.

The back door to the house opened, and a woman stepped out. She was about Mama's height, with the same dark hair. She wore a long dress like Mama's, too, that swished around her ankles as she came out carrying a bright light in one hand that shot beams into the distance.

Blinking, she shielded her eyes from the bright light. She didn't like it, and she couldn't see if this might be Mama with light shining right in her face.

"Bonjour?" the woman who might be Mama said. Did Mama know that word? *"Qu'est-ce que c'est ça? Une petite fille?"*

"Mama!" she called again, louder this time.

"C'est bon! C'est bon!" The woman rushed over, dropping the light and reaching for her.

This was not Mama.

But she sure smelled good.

And it had been a long time since she'd eaten.

With a wide smile on her face, she threw herself into the woman's arms, squeezed her tightly, and sunk her fangs right into her neck. The woman tried to scream, but ripping her throat out took care of that pretty quickly. Blood smeared her pretty dress, but Mama would understand. As quickly as she could, she lapped up the blood, noting it was much easier to kill this time than it had been. She felt stronger. She felt more powerful. Even when she'd finished licking her fingers of the last drops of blood, she felt hungrier.

"Mama!" she shouted, heading off toward the next light in the distance.

She didn't know where her mama was, but Bonnie was going to find her—one way or another.

Thank you for reading! Book 6 is coming soon!

ALSO BY ID JOHNSON

Stand Alone Titles
All I Want for Christmas is Pooch
(*sweet contemporary romance*)
Christmas Memory
(*sweet contemporary romance*)
Meet Cute Me Under the Mistletoe
(*sweet contemporary romance*)
The Doll Maker's Daughter at Christmas
(*clean romance/historical*)
Pretty Little Monster
(*young adult/suspense*)
The Journey to Normal: Our Family's Life with Autism (*nonfiction*)
Found by the Alpha (fantasy romance)

Love Throughout Time
(*time travel romance*)
Back to Titanic
Back to Gettysburg
Back to Bunker Hill

Back to the Highlands
Back to Port Royal

Silverwood Academy
(*paranormal romance*)
Vampire Hunter
World Builder
Realm Jumper

Celestial Springs
(*psychological thriller/literary fiction/women's fiction*)
Beneath the Inconstant Moon
The First Mrs. Edwards
Leaving Ginny

The Motherhood
(*dystopian romance*)
Rain's Rebellion
Rain's Run
Rain's Return

Ashes and Rose Petals
(*contemporary romance/retelling of Romeo and Juliet and Cinderella*)
Girl in the Attic
Girl From the Tomb
Girl On the Beach

Nashville Country Dreams
(*contemporary romance*)
Meant to Marry Me
Lead Me Home
You Are the Reason

Forever Love series

(clean romance/historical)
<u>Cordia's Will: A Civil War Story of Love and Loss</u>
<u>Cordia's Hope: A Story of Love on the Frontier</u>

The Clandestine Saga series
(paranormal romance)
<u>Transformation</u>
<u>Resurrection</u>
<u>Repercussion</u>
<u>Absolution</u>
<u>Illumination</u>
<u>Destruction</u>
<u>Annihilation</u>
<u>Obliteration</u>
<u>Termination</u>

A Vampire Hunter's Tale (based on The Clandestine Saga)
(paranormal/alternate history)
<u>Aaron</u>
<u>Jamie</u>
<u>Elliott</u>
<u>Christian</u>

The Chronicles of Cassidy (based on The Clandestine Saga)
(young adult paranormal)
<u>So You Think Your Sister's a Vampire Hunter?</u>
<u>Who Wants to Be a Vampire Hunter?</u>
<u>How Not to Be a Vampire Hunter</u>
<u>My Life As a Teenage Vampire Hunter</u>
<u>Vampire Hunting Isn't for Morons</u>
<u>Vampires Bite and Other Life Lessons</u>
<u>Gone Guardian</u>
<u>Death Does Not Become Her</u>

When You Say Nothing At All
My Girl
Unchained Melody
I Only Have Eyes For You
At Last
The Very Thought of You

Reaper's Hollow
(paranormal/urban fantasy)
Ruin's Lot
Ruin's Promise
Ruin's Legacy

When Kings Collide
(steamy historical romance)
Princess of Silence
Princess of Hearts

Collections
Ghosts of Southampton Books 0-2
Reaper's Hollow Books 1-3
The Clandestine Saga Books 1-3
The Chronicles of Cassidy Books 1-4
Celestial Springs Collection
Heartwarming Holidays Sweet Romance Books 1-3
Heartwarming Holidays Sweet Romance Books 4-7

Websites: https://books2read.com/ap/xX7ZD8/ID-Johnson

For updates, visit www.authoridjohnson.blogspot.com

Follow on Twitter @authoridjohnson

Find me on Facebook at www.facebook.com/IDJohnsonAuthor

Instagram: @authoridjohnson

Follow me on Bookbub: https://www.bookbub.com/authors/id-johnson